Street

Street

Tyler Stevens

 PaperBooks

Paperbooks Publishing Ltd, 2 London Wall Buildings,
London EC2M 5UU
info@legend-paperbooks.co.uk
www.legendpress.co.uk

Contents © Tyler Stevens 2010

The right of Tyler Stevens to be identified as the author of
this work has been asserted by him in accordance with the
Copyright, Designs and Patent Act 1988.

British Library Cataloguing in Publication Data available.

ISBN 978-1-9077563-5-1

*All characters, other than those clearly in the public domain, and
place names, other than those well-established such as towns and
cities, are fictitious and any resemblance is purely coincidental.*

Set in Times
Printed by Lightning Source, Milton Keynes
J. H. Haynes and Co. Ltd., Sparkford.

Cover designed by:
Gudrun Jobst
www.yotedesign.com

 **PaperBooks**

This is Tyler Stevens' first book.

1

There isn't a single person I've met that I haven't thought about killing or at least seriously harming. Take old Marvin down the road. Marvin's about sixty-four, I'd say. All the time he talked to me I couldn't stop thinking about his neck. How it was hanging, all that skin, and it flashed in my mind to properly gut the poor old fucker. He's none the wiser to this, and nor was he when I was thinking about booting him one in the face. I felt awful after that thought. No, seriously, I really did. What kind of kid thinks about booting an old man in the face when he's bending down to pick a coin off the floor? Terrible, I can tell you. Mind, I never did do Marvin in, but it got me thinking about things. How these thoughts started. Then something happened that made me go and get myself checked out.

One afternoon I had a smoke with one of the kids that sells dope for me, and he told me that he had been feeling funny. That he was thinking about doing someone in for no reason and he couldn't get it out of his head. It made me feel better knowing I wasn't the only one, and I got to thinking that maybe it was normal to have these thoughts as long as you didn't act on them. That you'd only act on them in a case of provocation. 'Provocation' – nice word that. I wouldn't use it for real, but it's nice to see it on the page here. Don't worry I'm just getting a few vocab rules right in my head, so I know what will be staying and going, then we can get on and write all this down properly.

So this kid, I'll call him Daren for now, it'll save a lot of grief from his family if this ever gets seen, tells me he's going to go into this day centre. Apparently he had heard you could just walk in, no note from the doctors, and tell them what's what. I was right into what he was saying and let him stay longer in the flat. I tried to get more out of him about his urges, all the while it was taking me every restraint – nice word that 'restraint', I'm going to use it properly I think – yeah, taking me all my time not to jump the fucker. Mad or what? I was looking at him, skinny runt, and I'm thinking, jump him now before he does you.

Daren left, and I heard from his cousin that he'd been into the day centre saying he was feeling strange and needed help. They discharged him the same afternoon after giving him some advice. A week later Daren got into an argument about a bag of pills and butchered the lad he was arguing with. Gutted him. Stabbed him sixty times. In broad daylight, he went into one over something trivial. He's now locked up in a mental hospital.

This thing with me, it comes and goes. Sometimes I don't feel like it at all. I go to work and nothing is a problem. I can talk to the girls in the office, go for a few beers, life's sweet. Then, and I haven't a clue how, it starts. And when it does, I can't listen to people when they're talking for thinking about doing them in. Friends, family, doesn't matter. I see their mouths moving and I'm looking at their necks thinking of the blood gushing out.

When I'm on the drink I try to shake my head, get the thoughts away, and I know I've let it slip a few times when I've been out with mates. I told one of them and he laughed it off and I very nearly gave it to him big time. And he's a pal, for Christ's sakes.

So I took today off work to go and see someone. I've looked this up and you've got to be careful because if I go in and spill the beans like I'm telling you, they can certify me a danger to the public and bang me up. And once you've been banged up as a nut, you're fucked for life. No job, no nothing. Can you imagine the stick off your pals about being a fruit?

And I've got a few things coming up. A few parties I'm supplying all the gear for, so it's big money. Money I could do with for a trip away. Trip away, you're thinking aaaaah, he's got it going on – you're right, I have. I'm going to be away out of this shit-hole of a country in no time. Money in pocket, drink in hand, on a golden beach with a big fat joint. Maybe not, though, it's all talk.

Another lad, a pal from way back, we've talked about hitting Thailand, doing it for a month. Something like that, but it's leaving things here, that's the problem. And I need these thoughts ironed out. I'm petrified in case I suddenly slip and start kicking people in the street who bend over to tie their shoelace. That would look alright, wouldn't it? Man in his suit bends over to pick his Parker pen up and yours truly spots him and runs over and boots him in the face. It's fucking hilarious, though, isn't it? The thought is, anyway, I'd be gutted to see him on his back. That's it, you see, I don't see any of the aftermath in my mind. I only get this urge to do it.

Today I took the day off to go and see a shrink. To tell him my problems. And I went and it was okay, except I knew he was messing with me, and he knew I was messing with him. I told him I felt out of sorts and sometimes violent. Tell me about the violent thoughts, he said. Queer looking fucker he was, long nose, thin, long legs, crossed, funny looking, like he was going to sneeze or fart at any second. I told him that if someone gets too close to me, like in a crowd, or right up to my face, I feel the urge to lash out. 'Lash out' – another good one that, I'll be using that again, sounds proper and right. It keeps the truth away from peering eyes.

What a bloke, though. All smarmy and knowing. I could have stood up and booted him just for the way he was crossing his legs. Thinking back, I should be praising myself for using such restraint, because if anyone was going to send you over the edge it was that tosser.

The shrink scribbled away and I told a pack of lies, which he got sick of and eventually gave me some advice, something like, Don't jump out in front of cars and don't head-butt trains, but feel free to punch as many bus drivers as you like. So I went straight out, got on the number thirty-nine and belted the fuck out of the woman driver. Absolute disgrace hitting a woman, I felt terrible, so I belted the nearest male passenger, booted him a good one and got off, shouting, Permission granted from the shrink!

Of course I didn't, but I might as well have. No wonder Daren let rip and spilled that kid if that was the type of advice he got. After that I went into town and messed around at the monument all afternoon. I got calls to sell a few deals, which I did in full view of everyone for some reason. I never sell outside the flat and only to regulars. Christ I've got a full time job, but today, I just didn't give a shit. I was officially mad and had a licence to fuck around.

On my way home I did something totally off the wall, which is why I'm standing at the window here, looking through the crack in the curtains at the flashing blue lights wondering if I've done anything else daft enough to get me some heat.

So what did I do? I'll tell you what I did. I invited a homeless person back to the flat for a bath and a shower and a decent feed.

She's in there now, scrubbing herself clean in my bath. Been in there for over an hour. Hilarious, or what? I don't know what came over me. Maybe I'm lonely, or it was an act of God. Fuck knows, but she's in there, up to fuck knows what.

Oh, here we go, knock, knock. There's someone at the downstairs door. I could blank it, but with the flashing blue lights and the guest in the bathroom and the shit load of dope I bought last night, I best get myself down and see what's happening.

2

My front door isn't what you'd call easily accessible from the outside. 'Accessible' – not as good a word as 'restraint', but it could come in handy when I'm telling this story proper, couldn't it? We'll put it in class two as a reserve word.

Looking at the back of the front door from the top of the stairs, this is what you see – nothing, it's too dark. Walk down a few steps and you see a steel plank across it. It's like the back of a barn door on those films when the enemy are trying to get in and they pull the plank down and lean against it. Except mine's steel and the slots it sits in are fixed to the floor. On top of that, in the centre, I have a t-piece which jams into the bottom step. The bottom step has a cross piece which is bolted to the walls either side, and a vertical support on the wall. Fort fucking knox or what? That dosser upstairs will shit herself when she comes out and sees that.

There was another knock, nothing heavy, more a, Are you in mate, knock, rather than a, Fucking open up we know you're a drug dealing murdering bastard, knock. So I blanked it and went back upstairs. I didn't look out of the window again. If they wanted in, that's where they'd be looking to see if I was a twitcher. And don't forget it's only just starting to get dark and I could still be at work for all these know. So they can't just come braying the door down when they feel like it. And I'm always careful getting my supplies in. I go once a week and only ever buy a 9-Bar. I don't know why I bother the dope market is fucked now. Years ago you'd get a ton or ton twenty for an ounce, now it's fifty or sixty, and people are still into skunk and the Albanians have got shit loads of skunk farms on the go around here. When I say farms, I mean empty flats rented to imaginary Albanians with real Albanians living underneath watching their money grow.

On top of it all I've become a victim of this credit crunch. People not having money goes all the way down the line. You've got three kids sharing a fiver deal on a Monday night instead of a tenner deal, which means less is smoked, and the kids buying off me don't come back as much. I'm shifting less and less and having to drop the price and this is all down to some bloke called Madoff. Fucking arsehole. If I saw him there may be a chance that I'd turn my thoughts into actions and gut him, see if any coin spills out of him, because apparently he took the world for 50bn. I couldn't give a fuck about that, what I'm bothered about is that I could end up working part-time and the dope price is in decline.

We're going to write all this down, this gutting business, see if we can get to the bottom of it. I've done twenty-two years already, so all being well, there'll be no volleying of unsuspecting shoppers' heads when they drop a five pence on the pavement. 'Pavement' – I know it's nothing special, but it feels special to me because I never wrote path. Pavement suggests I might be a bit, you know, well-read, or whatever.

So these parties, I'm trying to make a quick killing. In and out. Ketamine, horse shit, whatever these weirdoes are into I'm dishing up this weekend. The first do is at a mansion out in the country. Mummy and Daddy off on holiday probably. And these lot, apparently, are Goths. Have you seen Goths? I mean a load of them in all their gear? No wonder we used to go down to the monument and set about them when we were young. What a bunch of misfits. I saw one the other week with these huge biker boots on, moon walking, bouncing with every step. Big silver buckle on the front. Get a load together with their

Matrix trench coats and makeup on and you're in for a treat.

Goths at some mansion running around like crazy people, pumped full of E and Ketamine, ups and downs, loved up and psyched out. One of them must have a few quid because they're after a boat load of toot. Sounds good to me. One line of the marching powder and they just can't stop. They'll be on the blower every two minutes – Another gramme. Sorry can't deliver. We'll pay double. Not tonight Neeko. Treble. Might be able to do you one gramme. Drip feed them all night and like I said, I should make a killing. Sounds like I've done this before, but I haven't. I just sell harmless dope to subsidise my shit wages. 'Subsidise' – saw that on a memo at work. I'll have it, though, for this story. I just started selling to pals, and now I sell to a handful of people, and never after ten, so I'm not really a drug dealer – just a friend who has a bit left over for others – at a price.

To get this gig at the weekend I needed to produce some samples of all the products available. 'Products' – is going into a new category, along with 'Category', and it's going to be C. I would use them telling you what happened this weekend when I'm writing this down, but I wouldn't tell you straight up in conversation. I'd sound ridiculous. Talking of ridiculous, I just heard the last of the water drain down the plughole in the bath. We've got company.

3

She's called Veronica. I put her at forty. She kips down in the doorway of the old Pound Shop. The Pound Shop is still classed as town I would say. Not dead centre, sort of on the way out, but still the town. I'd class it as town and this is as close as she can get to all the punters knocking around at night to beg a few quid without going onto the main streets, where there's a good chance she'll get kicked to fuck on a regular basis. You get the odd dosser taking a chance, but there are hordes of piss-heads knocking about on weekends that would think nothing of toeing a beggar in the face en route to the next bar.

I've seen it before. This dosser had a dog with him for the sympathy vote and got volleyed in the face. Staying alive is hard for these people, especially in this freezing weather. Did I say it was two days before Christmas? There you have it. Season of good will and BOOT, one in the chops for you, pal.

Our guest is not as randomly selected as I made out earlier. When I pick the 9-Bar up on a Thursday night I have to go via her street. She's been there all summer, so I've dropped her a few quid here and there, when things were sweet. Before the banks and Madoff and interest rates fucked us all up. I've given her a twenty before. Big money that to the homeless. A twenty can last them a month. A couple of people do that and that's them flush through the summer or they can save up, and it will see them through the winter. So Veronica, if that's what she's called, she could have told me anything, who's bothered? Not me and not her. What are we to each other? Strangers who want nothing to do with each other. I have only stopped a few times because it was a nice night and I had nothing to go back to the flat for apart from half a joint in the ashtray and some shit TV.

I think the first time I stopped, she asked me for a light so I tossed her a lighter. She took so long lighting the dump I told her to keep it and walked away. Don't look at me like that. You'd fucking walk away. Our Veronica is not a looker. I'm not saying she's ugly, but what you can see under the layers of filthy scarves, hats and second hand coats is not exactly appealing. Well, it wasn't then, when I first gave her that lighter.

The next few Thursdays I just nodded and kept

on walking, and anyway, as far as I can remember, the weather was bad. Cold and raining. The British summer. You honestly think I'd talk about the weather? I will when I tidy this story up. Like those other writers, the good ones, I'm going to slip a bit of scenery into the story, make it more real, so you lot can feel what's happening, when it happens.

So, I'd drop her the odd fiver, and I'd stop and have a smoke if the weather was alright. She was interesting, Veronica. Not what you'd expect. She wasn't like over the top about getting a fiver, just, Cheers mate. And she wasn't grumbling about her life being shit. She was alright about things. And one thing I noticed, which was strange for a dosser, and no I'm not a connoisseur of dossers – 'Connoisseur', that'll have to be cut from the final edition, it's too much to do with food. I'm no expert on dossers, but her teeth were immaculate. Whiter than yours and mine. Her face would be scruffy and I've never seen her hair, but her teeth – pearly white. Which made it easier to talk to her. Her mouth always looked fresh and clean, like of one of those toothpaste adverts. And like I said, she wasn't a moaner.

Where she slept wasn't far from the park and she could see a few benches that were just in the light of the street lamps. She always had something to tell you. Not straight away, she'd start off going on about the fumes off the buses, just how black they were making the pavements and the amount of pollution that was coming out of them. It wasn't moaning, it was more a debate she was having with herself and if I had anything to say I would. And those benches were a source of entertainment for her. Her TV. Drunks falling out of the Horse Shoe and wanking each other off, birds giving blow jobs left right and centre. That's how I knew she was older, she thought nothing of laughing about a bird sucking someone off. 'Proper going down on him, should have seen t'face on him.' I forgot to mention, she's from Yorkshire somewhere.

Veronica has been on the street a while, I reckon. She doesn't carry a lot of stuff like the newcomers. The newcomers have got mountains of bags. All fucking right, I'm a connoisseur of the homeless. And find me another word to replace 'Connoisseur'. Come to think of it, I am a bit of a street roamer, aren't I? I do enjoy having a stroll about. The plan is that by the end of this story, I'll be sorted. One way or t'other – T'other. That's how Veronica speaks. It's great. T'other way, mate. T'other day I were... absolute scream. I tell you what though, we're going to have to find another word for 'Connoisseur'. I'm not having that.

And here's one for you, and I'm not sure how this stacks up against my current problem, but I

can't remember ever wanting to do Veronica in.
Maybe I did, but forgot. And look at the position
she's always in. Could be because all I can see is
her face, or mouth, and she's looking up at me. No
hanging flesh or bending over in front of me or
getting too close. I think everyone must have a
'getting too close' zone. Must have. That invisible
force field where if an uninvited guest comes
inside of it you want to nut the living daylights out
of them. I'm not alone on this I'm sure of that.
There are hundreds certified and in padded cells,
but look at me, free as a pigeon to shit where I want
and think nothing of it.

Here we go, V the dosser is opening the
bathroom door. Any luck and she's turned into a
stunner.

4

No such luck. I'll tell you what, though, she looks better for a good clean up. She's standing there, head hanging to the side, drying her hair, which is blonde, I think. Hard to tell with it still being wet. She's thin, only wearing a vest and not a hint of a pair of tits. Nothing to get excited about there. Why am I bothered? As if I'm going to jump her like some kind of sex pest. Hardly. I'm doing the old doll a favour, getting her spruced up before turfing her back out into the snow. I bet sleeping in snow isn't that bad. Compacted down nice and hard, decent sleeping bag and you'd be laughing. Got to be better than rain, hasn't it?

Veronica stood up and walked towards me and I felt a rush of blood to my face. After the day I'd had, what with the shrink, the police outside, and now a complete stranger standing in one of my towels, I swear I'm as close as I've ever been to doing something.

I got out of it by walking into the kitchen and

asking Veronica if she wanted something to eat. And she did, if it wasn't too much trouble. Her Yorkshire accent got me smirking and I loosened up as I went about putting some food on.

While I had been cooking in the kitchen, trying not to think of a stranger in my flat and all this shit going on, Veronica had rolled two cigarettes and came over to the breakfast bar. She used my lighter to light them both up and handed me one. Looking at her, I'm not sure how old she was now. She wasn't forty and she wasn't twenty, and like I said, she had whiter than white teeth. This is the kind of stuff I need to get down when I'm telling this story for it to be right.

I dished the food up and Veronica got stuck in. Not like a savage or anything, she just ate well, and who could blame her? As she was finishing her meal, I found myself staring at the bread knife on the table. I had used it to cut the pizza in four.

Veronica, who I would now say was about twenty-six and Jewish, was rabitting away, on about stuff that had happened on the benches last night. Nothing smutty, mind. I think she would have been thinking I'd take it the wrong way if she had started going on about people at it in the park. I probably would, except I wouldn't jump Veronica if there were only her and I left in the world. Well

I probably would, but I wouldn't be happy about it.

I picked the knife up, put it on my plate, and took it into the kitchen. Out of sight, out of mind. Then I got thinking that by tomorrow, all this could pass again, because that's happened before. I've tried to remember what life was like then, compared to now, to see if circumstances were different so I can find out what brings it on, but I can't. All I know is that Veronica isn't safe in here. I thought she was, but after the knife thing and when she bent over for the towel... I needed her out.

When Veronica came out of the bathroom, I told her to have a smoke. I had plenty on the table. She sat down with her back to me and started talking. Honestly, her accent will crack you up. I mean she's funny as hell and the Yorkshire accent is so strong it's a dream. You want to hear her? Here you go,

'So, for this t'work, Tyler, you need to be tough and not t'think of weather and get all sentimental wu me. So I think it best if I just do one after this smoke, oright?'

So Veronica with her pearly whites and single gold tooth. Did I mention the tooth? How is this going to be a good account of things if I miss details like that out? She's got one gold tooth that makes her look like a rasta or a hippy, and to be fair, looking at her there now in just a blue vest and

jeans, hair hanging over the side of her face as she
rolls cigarette after cigarette, there is something
attractive about her. I'm not saying I'd be into her
or anything, but V looked street. 'Street'. What
does that mean? It's a saying I've just made up to
mean on the ball, out there, in amongst it, at ease,
on the level. Our V is street.

I walked over and checked out the window and
they had gone. No flashing blue lights, which
meant I was in the clear to drop off the samples for
the parties at the weekend. Which, of course, was a
nice excuse to get rid of V. So I told her I had a few
things to do and she went on and on about how I
didn't need to make stuff up, that she was going
anyway and wouldn't have stayed if I had begged
her. I nearly said, Fuck off, you would stay all night
if I let you, soaking up heat and filling up on pizza
and chips to last you a week, but I used restraint –
I'll point this out now so this doesn't get tedious. If
one of these posh words slips in when I'm telling
you what's what, I won't mention it, alright? I'll try
not to anyway. Me and you know why it's there,
which category it has come from, and if I get the
chance to change things later, after the story, I will,
but that's what I'm scared of. Not getting back to
the pen and paper here when this weekend is over.
You know that, though, right? Why else would I
talk to you like this if I knew for sure that I was

going to get back in time to change everything and make it just so? It's the thoughts, isn't it? I know they're stronger than ever and with this weekend coming up I haven't got time to sort everything out. I can't even lock myself away, and the fact that I've went and brought a complete stranger into my flat for no reason and I've got to get shot of her for own safety... is, well, worrying to say the least.

By the time I had my coat, hat and gloves on, Veronica was already ahead of me dressed in twenty layers, and I heard her shout, 'Whoa, what's w' all security, Tyler?'

I came up behind her and said, 'I'm going to slit your throat, I'm afraid, so you best accept it and let us get on with it.'

Course I didn't say that, but my face was blazing and I needed to be out. I told her it wasn't such a good area and after a couple of break-ins I had gone overboard. I opened the door and we stepped out into a blizzard and the two of us were blown back on our heels and we both started laughing. V linked my arm and we pushed against the storm, snow whipping into our faces from all angles. We were covered in seconds, and V had shrunk to three feet tall as I more or less pulled her up the road. There were a couple of cars crawling up the bank and I lifted my head slightly and I was blinded.

We made it to the corner of the road and then we

were out of it. We were like two snowmen, laughing and smiling. I very nearly put my arm round her, all jubilant I was, but she walked away, waving as she went into her doorway.

I stood, suddenly feeling lonely, like the train had just pulled out of sight. I turned around, looking back at where we had come from. Not a single person around, and the parked cars were covered with snow that must have been two feet deep, like on a Christmas card or cartoon. Then I remembered the meeting with the two Goths and headed off towards the park.

5

I arrived at Leazer's Park ten minutes late. A beautiful park, especially during the day. Winding footpaths, tennis courts, and the lake, which had recently been drained and re-filled. Word had it there were enough needles in there to supply the general hospital for the next century. Fucking junkies. The place is rife with them. You couldn't get a stranger set up than this park. Kids playing on the grass or in the kids' play area, old men with their grandkids feeding the ducks and swans, and in the bushes, junkies shooting up. That's the world over though, isn't it? They say you're only ever a metre away from a rat. I'm not just talking about the furry ones you put poison down for. World's fucked.

I just hope these two make-upped clowns don't get all leery. Really, I should have something on me. Something to pull out of the inside of my jacket and crack the fuckers over the head with should they so much as fucking blink. But you know as well as I do, the way things are with me, that would be fatal. So I'm here with nothing but a bag of gear. A pick-and-mix of toot, ketamine, acid, dope and E. No skunk. Couldn't get any apart from off the Albanians and I don't want to get into that caper.

Like the abominable snowman, I came round the corner and into the park. Not a soul. And the snow was still coming down heavy, covering everything. I kept to walking around the lake, just outside the line of the street lamps.

A friend of a friend organised this and the more I thought about it, the more it looked like a set-up. Could be the law or to turn me over. Either way, what was I doing down here in this weather? I couldn't do a runner, didn't have anything to defend myself with and a pocket full of gear. I've never done anything like this before, and here I am on my own, circling the lake waiting for a leper to jump out of the bushes with a needle and take me down. The only consolation was the hospital opposite, all lit up. Filled with ill people and I'd be able join them. If anyone bothered to take me.

I leant back against the wooden hut. You couldn't see it now, because of the snow, but in daylight, it was green. It looked tatty, but nice. In the summer you can get an ice-cream from this hut and a cup of coffee. Ideal if you're hanging about waiting for someone to croak it, or you're taking one of your friends off the ward for a joint. No better place, and everyone else is at it. All except the crack heads in the bushes puncturing their veins.

A couple of minutes passed and I was about to do one, get the hell out of there and never look back at such a crazy idea, when I spotted the two Goths. How had I missed them? Standing right next to the entrance to the park on the hospital side, in their moon boots, sharing a smoke. You could see them perfectly under the light, and it made me think of a couple of cows. You know, black and white jerseys. Except these cows could stand up, and they had the mannerisms of humans. A couple of upright cows covered in chains and shit smoking under the light. I headed over.

More cows came through the park entrance covered in chains, black and white, stamping their feet and rubbing their hands. Park cows. Take any bunch of Goths and replace the background you see them in with two green hills and a few scattered sheep, and there you have it.

My herd were gathering round a lamppost and were probably high off all the dog piss that had been splattered up it all day. I turned and looked down at the lake and the island in the middle. What a postcard that would make. An ice rink, a big circle right there in front of me, not a single footprint, just waiting to be run over or a snowman built out of it.

I thought about building a snowman just then. If I'd had time I think I would have, but it gave me a heavy heart. You know what I mean? What he represents, built out of snow and standing all alone, made me feel empty and low thinking of building that snowman.

I was sheltered from all sides and the snow that did come from above was filtered through a tree. I pulled my hood back and lifted my head up. Before I knew it I had my mouth open catching snowflakes on my tongue. I titled my head forward, all happy I was, and watched the wind rush along the footpath from the top of the park like it was chasing someone. Whoosh! It went down the path, crossing over the lake, whipping up the snow in its wake. Yet the snow behind it didn't seem to settle down. It was up and up and the storm was wild, not knowing which way to go, looking one way then the other.

The storm chased something down the steps and out onto the road. What a spot this was for watching nature go at it. I'm telling you this snowstorm was angry. If this storm had been thinking like me, it would have picked me up and smashed me onto the frozen lake and cracked my head open, then flung me into the trees before rushing off into the night like a ghost dashing along streets looking for someone to spook.

This storm was a nasty fucker and I watched nature shit itself there and then. And I didn't blame it. Got me thinking that maybe I might go back via the main road so there were people about. The storm couldn't give a fuck about that, and who was I kidding, frightened of a storm?

I came out of my hiding spot, round the corner, and walked over to the two Goths.

6

I came out of the bushes and shadows at a decent pace, and as I did, one of them stepped back and they fell silent. I kept on walking, not making eye contact and said, all James Cagney like, 'Let's take a walk.'

And off I went down the bank, one hand in my pocket on the gear, the other hanging loose, the two Goths following me. Ahead was the lake and we were walking into the storm, not as bad as the high street, but it was pushing us back. Someone over the far side had stopped and turned back, the force of Old Storm sending them packing. I didn't know where I was headed and these two behind me must have been thinking, What the fuck is he up to? But I didn't know what else to do. I couldn't just stand there and have a friendly chat under the street light in full view of the hospital, could I?

We passed an opening and I glanced over at the hospital and could see steam or something coming off a generator. There were two generators at the corner of two buildings, tucked away in an L-shape. It must have been emergency supplies or something, and it was dark in there. Well, half of it was, the other half catching some of the light from the car park, and the snow was being whipped against the wall, covering it halfway down.

To think that thousands of people's lives could count on those generators. They were a decent size. I'd say the size of two cars, tail-to-tail, and another two cars stacked on top. That was the size of them and the smoke puffing out made me feel all warm. I thought about hot dogs and Hansel and Gretel, and getting my head down for the night, all warm in the flat.

'Everything still on, brother?'

I turned and faced the two Goths. Up close they weren't so radical, that was just me being racist. They had piercings a-plenty, but they weren't too bad. The one doing the talking was tall, too tall, and too close. I lifted my hand up and outstretched it as far as I could to see if I could touch him. I couldn't. Fucker never flinched. Probably thought I was off my head. Never mind. Doing business where we stood was impossible with Old Storm trying to throw us in the lake.

'Which one of you is Damien?'

The tall one, black hair sticking out the bottom of his woolly hat, nice long trench coat and plenty

37

mascara. I think it was mascara, some shit around the eyes. His mate, shorter, about my height, had a skinhead and was wearing no hat. I looked at him and said, 'Where the fuck's your hat?'

'It blew off on the way up here.' He smiled and looked at his friend.

Damien, my contact, nodded. 'It did. Everything – okay? Simon sort everything with you okay, brother?'

Brother. He deserved a crack just for that. When young kids meet a dealer, they try to be all street. They aren't street like our V, who has to try and show that she is less street than she is. They want to be on the dealer's level – nothing the bother, brother.

I got them to follow me further around the lake and I spotted a man and woman down at the bus stop. Can you believe that? Two foot of compacted snow, it hadn't let up in hours, cars left stranded sticking out in the road, and there was a couple standing in the bus stop. They were all wrapped up, bags of Christmas shopping, probably warmed up with a few straight whiskies before they left town. I was fascinated watching the two of them, worriedly checking their watches and then standing out in the road to see if the bus was chugging along. When the man came back into the bus stop he had an inch of snow on him, head-to-toe, yet he still believed a bus driver would be coming along soon. What a scene.

I went down a set of stairs, up another, and eventually sat down on a bench with my back to Old Storm. The two Goths sat down next to me. I apologised for all the James Bond stuff. I made an excuse up about meeting someone else at the same time, and they bought it. I told Damien that everything was on the level, and gave him the gear he had ordered and took the cash. I gave him my mobile and said I'd meet him tomorrow, same time same place, then I called him Sixes. Damien-Three-Sixes, and I smirked and so did he. He liked that. So I told Sixes, that only he was to contact me. He was in the know with a big time dealer – we were now blood brothers and he'd be getting the best deals around. They both fucked off and so did I, but I couldn't help looking back at the park.

No people, but so much going on. And where were the ducks and swans when Mother Nature was letting rip? Where were they? I sat back down, my heart thumping, getting all hyper about some ducks and nature and shit that I wouldn't dream of before, and now because I wasn't feeling like myself, I had nature on my fucking shoulders. Like Madoff hadn't left me enough to deal with.

I could have burst into tears. Not bother writing this down and just fuck off and let happen what's going to happen. Fighting it had got me worn out, and look at the lake for Christ's sakes, it's like a fucking tornado. They're all in on the act, even the trees, bending in unison, one way then the other. Old Storm's in charge, he's conducting proceedings. He doesn't care who wants to do what, he's calling the shots and the place is rocking. Whoosh one way, whoosh the other. Aren't you all fancy now the park is empty? But I'm here watching, don't you know? I'm here too.

I watched a while longer trying to chill out. When the hopelessness of what I was trying to do got to me, I could roll over into a tight ball and hope life would get on without me.

I thought back to when I was standing in the bar trying to keep a straight face when that man bent over in front of me after dropping his change. I was giddy, just about a hopeless case I was, trying not to boot him in the face. I'll tell you what's even funnier, if I play that scene a bit longer and then pause it – the look on everyone's face. Try it. Slow motion, boot, up the head comes, frowns come down, jaws drop open, women drop glasses, his head flies back and I'm laughing uncontrollably, like someone has spiked me with laughing pills. Fast forward and by God would it kick off. The piece of magic, that golden moment, was the look on their faces, and that's what got me thinking like this all the time. I'm sure that was the start and I haven't been able to get back to when I never saw those faces. I don't know what's changed so much. I really don't.

7

Old Storm was hot on my heels and I threw my hat at him. Go on you mad fucker! You'll not do me! I ran and slipped over, but the snow was made for falling on. It was real snowball snow, know what I mean? If it had been walked on and trampled down, like out on the road, you could have grabbed a gas board from one of the thousands of holes around town, jump on it, and been away down the road.

I was on the ground looking down into the park and I could see the eye of Old Storm, going one way then the other, like an angry ghost. I'm telling you it's the ghost of Christmas past or some shit, running down stairs, into bushes, rustle, rustle, any junkies? I'll check further up. I only hope he doesn't start picking the used needles up and tossing them about like he is doing with the snow because I'll look like fucking Hell Raiser, what a scene! What a scene – how ironic – would-be drug dealer, just before Christmas, begging for mercy from Mother Nature, scrambling away from a Stephen King creation, and Old Storm lets ten syringes go into his face. What justice!

Christ, what a manic night.

I got to my feet and I felt elated – steady, I can't let that go, can I? And it's been a while since we added to our acceptable vocabulary for the final cut, so 'elated' goes in class two. I like the word a lot, because it makes me feel white and bright, like the backend of a storm has blown right through me.

I hope I see this through. I really do, because I'm going to come back to this park, one year from now, or whenever we get snow like this again, and I'm going to wait for Old Storm to come back and I'm going to thank Mother Nature. Oh, yes I am, and I think I'll bring myself a flask and a couple of pre-rolled joints and get set up for the night and watch it all happen again, because let me tell you this was better than any TV show. The Goths. Sixes and his baldy friend, the dense man and woman desperate to get home, and my friend, Old Storm, putting a theatrical show on. It made me feel so good.

I came out of the park and crossed the road, skidding on the snow. Normally you would expect some slush where the cars and gritters had been, maybe some tarmac showing, but it was solid and I've could've rolled around in it.

As I came to the top of the road, I felt like a quick drink. Just one pint, and I could see the pub ahead. There were lights on, but the window was covered with snow. The Blue Bell sign was an inch thick with the stuff, swinging peacefully in the wind. Another postcard from Santa's grotto.

I walked past a man trying to push his car. His wife, all fur-coat and hat, was at the wheel trying not to spin it. The fur stuck in my mind, and even though the man glanced up for help, I just walked straight past. Fucking fur coat. Get out and walk, you murdering cow.

I got to the pub door, heard all the chat, and walked away. Hurried away. All agitated again, and honestly I could have gone in there and done the lot of them. All happy red faces full of wine and sweet mince pies, plenty money in the bank, jobs safe, they're alright. Fucking work pals. Who needs them? Not me. Back stabbers, work pals. You work with the fuckers every day and you think you know them. They pour their hearts out to you when they split up with their girlfriends, but you tell me how many work friends you stay in touch with when they go to another company? Exactly. The lowest of the low. Back stabbers, worst ever. My only regret is that I didn't see it coming. Fuck me, I feel hysterical.

Another car on the mini roundabout had been abandoned. I thought about the dense couple at the bus stop, and I smiled, then laughed. Life wasn't so bad, you know. I just needed to step on the right stones to get across the lake. How poetic was that? That'll be in the final version for sure. I might even bookmark the page when I leave it on the table so they read that and think, This kid had brains you know. A little mixed up, but there was culture there.

That little sentence just there about the stones made me feel good and I got up and thought, You know what? I'm going to pop round and see V. Why not? We're friends, she's probably expecting me.

8

When you're in a hurry to get somewhere it always takes longer than if you're dawdling. If you're dawdling, all the time in the world, you don't care. And after marching head on into the storm taking the quickest route to V's place – V's place, you'd think I was going to a nice establishment with a roaring fire wouldn't you? Lady Veronica waiting, swirling brandy round her glass, admiring all the Christmas cards she had been sent, strung out beautifully on the wall above the fire. It would have to be an open fire, crackling away, and I'd settle on the big rug on the floor, leaning up on one elbow. I'd probably have a sherry. Would I fuck. Sherry? Fuck me, I once had an aunty who drank sherry. QC sherry and she'd down it by the bottle. I called in to see her one day and I saw an empty bottle lying under the sofa. She hadn't even noticed and there was another bottle already opened on the side board. A nice woman who enjoyed a tipple. I think she's dead now. I heard something or other about her dying, but I can't remember for sure. Did she die? Must have. I would have only been about nine last time I seen the old bat, so yeah, stick her down as departed. Departed old sherry drinker.

Anyway, where was I? Oh, yeah, so I stopped being in a hurry. There was no need. The more I fought against Old Storm the harder it became. That's what I'm saying, the harder you try, the worse it gets, and let's face it, it's not like V would be anywhere other than huddled up in her doorway, is it?

I sidestepped the wind for a second and stood in an alley. I had a foot of snow on me. I tell you what I would have looked like to a passerby, had anyone been game enough to come out in this weather. I would have looked as if I'd fallen down the side of a cliff, or been one of these radical snow boarders who'd tumbled down a mountain bouncing of rocks and landed with ten foot of snow on top of me. You couldn't see me for the stuff, and I found it quite funny, but I tell you what, and this is a funny feeling, I didn't fancy getting warm and cleaned up. You know how you can't wait to get in and get sorted out, clothes off, on the radiator, leave your big socks on until you warm up? I wasn't up for that at all. I was already warm, and enjoying being out in the snow. I had this urge to go back to the park and watch things going on.

I just didn't want to go home. With V gone, I was frightened I'd become lonely. I liked her being around, a friend to chat to, and now me, on my own messing about trying to get reception on the TV and smoking joints. One thing for sure, when I did go back, the heating would be staying on all night. Fuck the bills. When I left the next tenant was welcome to them. Council tax, the lot. Get that down you, pal. You get fuck all for doing things right. You might as well join the scum bag crew and not pay your bills. Offer to give them 50p a year until you head off into the sunset with the old sherry drinker. Why not? How many people get taken to court for not paying council tax now? Not many, and electricity is worse. I've never heard of anyone getting their collar felt for that. So why pay it? Especially when you've been singled out through no fault of your own to go on the scrap heap.

All the time I had been standing there, there was a man or woman, I couldn't tell through the snow, standing at the entrance to the Black Bull. Old Storm had decided to come up from the park into the town square and start looking in the shop windows. He whipped round the monument and darted over to the Blue Bell and looked in the window. Nothing doing, across the square, blasting the snow up into the air. You couldn't see your hand in front of your face.

I stepped out into the street, turning my shoulder and head to the side, like I was pushing a truck, leaning right into it. If Old Storm suddenly disappeared, I'd hit the deck. I was making progress across the road, trying to sneak a look at who was in the doorway.

It was impossible to see, and when I tried to look, I got it right in the eyes. I pushed on, curious as to who stands outside in this weather smoking. If they were a chain smoker, then why not head home and smoke in peace? I would, if I needed that much nicotine inside me, I'm telling you I'd be at old V's, swirling the brandy and getting my bare feet as close to the open fire as I could, not standing out in this shit. Anyway, I made it to the corner of the shops, then felt my way along the wall.

9

When I got to the entrance to the Black Bull there was no one there. Hardly a disappearing act, nothing mysterious enough for Sherlock and his sidekick to get involved with, he had probably gone back inside, and I don't blame him.

Inside the doorway, I loosened off a bit, down with the scarf, hood off, flexed my back. There were about 600 cigarette dumps on the floor. Some squashed with the ends torn off and others left to burn out but only getting so far along because of the wet floor. I wouldn't care, there was one of those outdoor ashtrays on the wall. You know the ones you see at McDonalds, or outside plush bars, where you can stub it out and then drop it in? No use at the Black Bull though. This was an Old Fart's bar. It's beyond me how a place that is practically city centre can stay open when hardly any fucker goes in at night. You get the daytime zombies getting tanked up on a pound a pint, shuffling two doors down to the bookies and back, but fuck me how can you make money on that? You can't. The landlord in here will be a dealer. A real scum bag punting Es to ten-year-olds all day long and any other shit he can get his hands on.

I was beginning to see why the chain smoker before me had stayed out so long. Old Storm could do his worst out there, any which way he wanted, but here, not a single drop. Well maybe just a little, but it didn't bother me, standing here smoking, watching the Blue Bell across the road. I can't be on thinking about them in that Blue Bell. Brings me so far down I could be sick. And why should I let them still be doing that to me?

I'm off to see V. Or should I have one in The Bull? I tell you what. If it's full I'll get a double vodka, down it, and we'll go see V. Failing that, a pint with a chaser, bit scout about and then go and see V.

I opened the door. One kid playing on the bandit. Skinny fucker in a golf jumper. Not that he would be playing much golf. He'll be out skelping cars as soon as the weather calmed down. Past him there were a couple of old men sitting, half a pint a piece, one nodding, one talking. Not much wrong with that.

I stood inside the doorway and leant on the counter at the bar, where there was a sign saying,

Order Food Here. I know this is a dump, but I bet they serve decent grub and at anytime of the day. Not like some of these fancy places, these, Meet after work and fill your face on six quid bits of fluffy pastry places. The food would be nice in here, and I decided right then, that tomorrow, after V, and after I'd tried to get my head down for the night, I'd be coming here. In with the other fuck-ups and pensioners to have a good feed.

The barman came over and I ordered a pint of larger with a Jack Daniels and coke. As I did, the car thief on the bandit dropped a few quid and a grin crawled up the side of his face. He'll know that fruit machine inside out, when it's going to drop and when it's not. It's just a matter of if he had thieved enough money today to keep going before he gets unlimited nudges or the feature.

He has no competition. All the coffin dodgers are interested in is being out the house, because it does them good to get out. Normally I'd take the piss, but I know how they feel. My flat is like a big black cloud today. Since V and me left, it's been there in the back of mind nagging away, and if I go back there, I've got to finish writing things down, and if I do that and I haven't got anywhere, you know, not got any help or something, then it'll be over, and I'll not know what to do.

So I apologise for rambling about this pub, it's

just that V's my last stop, and that's it until I've got to meet the Goths, and I know V will think there's something up if I talk to her too long in this weather. If I had my way, I'd bunk down with her tonight. Have a sleep over at hers, the two of us tucked up in the doorway of The Pound Shop. We'd probably have a good night you know. Look at what it was like down the park, it was amazing. Better than a TV show, and there's plenty goes on in V's park, we'd have a great laugh.

I downed the whiskey first, caught the barman's attention and ordered two more. Separate glasses, mate, just singles, what do you think I am, a fucking alky, you drip? And he was, mind. A proper one, teeth you could peel apples on and they desperately needed a brush. He would have to go to town on them with a car waxer or something to get any sort of result.

After demolishing a carrot he came over and asked me what was up, and I said, nothing, just needed a bit of a warm through. He said it was quiet if I wanted to come through to the lounge. Fucking lounge. It wasn't like there were people in suits and 1970s women in long red dresses leaning over the tables singing the blues. The lounge meant the seating was a slightly better quality, not so many knife rips.

I shouldn't say that. He was only being helpful.

I called him back over, ordered another whiskey, told him to get one, and thanked him. I said I was feeling a bit off, you know with Christmas and shit. He nodded. Knew the feeling well, he said... then his voice tailed off and all I could see was his big Adam's apple shooting up and down as he pulled the pint. Up and down like a fucking turkey and this wasn't a boot in the face type neck, the turkey barman with the gamy teeth needed gutting.

I could see the blade, kitchen knife, mine, silver, thick, enough to hack his whole head off if I wanted, but just a good go at it, would do fine.

The bandit freak dropped some change and as he bent over, I turned away and spat my mouthful of beer across the bar. I couldn't keep the laugh in. I turned away towards the door, fucking hysterical, trying desperately not to think of the look on his face after I had booted him. I'm seeing the smirk slip up the side of his face, followed by total disbelief after being toed in the face. I've got it on freeze frame and I can't stop laughing, fuck me, never, ever, will you see a funnier look than bandit freak after being booted.

The old men had homed in on me and bandit freak was standing with his back to the pillar, talking to the barman about me and I don't blame them. Fucking weirdo bursting out laughing like I had tourettes. I downed the last shot of whiskey, slipped the glass into my pocket and walked out the door. Time to see V.

10

My stomach was flipping over and over as I approached V's doorway from the side street. I had laughed just about every second of the way, one of those laughs where you need to hurry off to a corner, somewhere out of sight, and hope you don't throw up you're laughing so hard. Bandit freak's face was too much to take on board and now I had to blank him out. If I didn't, V wouldn't be too happy. Who would? It's funny when you see someone laughing. You know, on TV, when some newsreader gets the giggles, it's just about impossible not to laugh with them. Well this is what I had, but after ten minutes laughing like this in someone's face, they'll get freaked out.

I went down on one knee, holding my side. A stitch or something, and I felt ill, then I remembered the whiskey, and you know what? I've never drunk whiskey in my life. Not once. It was the scene, you see? The bar, the stale smell and the noise of the fruit machine and the barman from the

Texas Chain-saw Massacre family, made me go all American and buy whiskey.

The smell had me retching, so I stuck my fingers down my throat and the lot came scooting out all over the beautiful white snow. I had given Old Storm the slip. The snow was falling peacefully, so I tilted my head back again, like I had down the park. Just the job after throwing up, nice, wet and cold, and the sky was white. I walked ahead a few paces and looked around at everything covered in beautiful whiteness, and I breathed in, a nice big one. All that goodness and beautifulness, and I felt elated again, top of the world!

I strode on, all full of it, V's door just ahead, and I decided to play a joke, get her in the mood, see if she was up for a laugh. I got to the side of The Pound Shop. I listened to see if I could hear her moving around or talking to herself. I'd heard her doing that a few times, probably just to keep warm, but it's enough to have a laugh about when you're good mates. I think we've come far enough for me to be able to play a joke on her, haven't we?

I bent over and pulled my boot off, stood up, resting my foot on my other boot. Then, like a soldier throwing a grenade into a bunker, I flung the boot along and kept out of sight. Now this doorway is deep. You know, like a jewellers, with windows either side before you get to the main door. That's why V loves it, keeps her nice and warm. When the other dossers are running for cover in the underground car parks, V stays put, no matter what the weather. Even Old Storm would run out of puff before he could get right up to V.

No response, she must have been flat out. I came out of hiding, hopping round the corner and stepping into the doorway. She wasn't there. I tell you what though, Old Storm had had a good go. He had been half way down and it must have been too much for her.

My boot had landed just where the snow had stopped. I knelt down and started putting it back on. I tied my lace, right up around the side, because I'd be out in this a while longer. Maybe all night.

As I was finishing tying it in a double knot I noticed all the black on the snow. Like gravy or something. Just along from where I was kneeling. It was all down one side, this gravy or oil, right up to the entrance. And the snow had been trodden down in the doorway, so she must have only just left. I looked at where she usually slept, and there was more.

I walked further along onto the concrete and up to the shuttered door, which was covered in it. Splattered right up the door, the side and on the wall below the window. I leant back against the door, knees together, and dropped down, looking out into the snow.

I looked to the side and this oil was up the wall. I looked above where I was sitting and it was there. There was a small pool of it next to my boot, and like the fucking clown I am, I put my finger in it and tasted it. I jumped up – fuck me, it was blood. Fuck me, it was blood, proper panic stations. I was out of there like a shot. V's blood on the floor. She'd been done in. Done over, some cunt done her, look at all the fucking blood, Jesus fuck, what a mess!

I ran into the park, not knowing what to do, my mind going crazy jumping from the couple at the bus stop full of hot toddies to the bandit freak rolling V for what she had. I ran into the middle of the park, Old Storm had found me, and I fell to my knees and burst into tears. Screamed at the sky, ripped my hat off and threw myself face down, beating the ground, screaming V's name. Why would anyone do this at Christmas? Why would anyone do this at Christmas? The heartless bastards! I jumped to my feet and grabbed lumps of snow, throwing them into the dark. Fuck you! Fuck your storm! I let rip, throwing like crazy, hoping that every fucker from work would be down there, catching them in the face until they couldn't take no more. I kept doing it and doing it, until I burnt out.

A proper moment that was and I'm in tears and I don't know why. And I want it to stop. I want these thoughts to go away. I hold my hands up, the dosser getting a kicking upset me. I've just had the old girl in for a bath and a feed. I don't want to be alone tonight. I can't be alone and I know I'm not safe. No one is.

A man walking his dog shouted over at me and I got up of my hands and knees. Waved at him to let him know I was okay. I was one of these new snow boxers that were in training for the next big one.

I got up, all giddy again, and ran down the park, kept on at a good gallop, until I reached the first park bench, the light shining on it like that scene from The Warriors. You ever seen that film? 1970s gangs fighting and one gang member – just like what I'm looking at now, except my scene is very 1960s and black and white – gets talking to a prostitute and the pro turns out to be a copper and chains him to the seat. Remember? That's what I walked up to, out of the darkness and into a black and white movie.

11

It was like walking on stage when I came out of the dark and up to the bench. I felt like raising my arms... Thank you, thank you, please, quieten down and let us begin. What made it extra special was that the next spotlight further along was out, everything around it dark except for the singer, twirling round the lamppost, flitting from one side of the stage to the other.

I've got to have this scene in the final cut, but what for? Nothing happens here, but it looks so good. Straight ahead you can see twenty yards, then it's pitch black... Along the footpath you see a little further, then a black patch, where the light is out, then nothing. A vulnerable situation that made me feel excited, waiting for something to happen. Someone to come out of the dark.

They came from behind, the scene could be. Me lighting a cigarette, them knowing I'm distracted, and round the neck with a garrotte. I wouldn't even struggle, I'd just let them get on with it. Fill their boots. It would be out of my hands then. My fate would be sealed and the stomach cramps would be gone. Wiped out, just like that. Is it all worth saving? Was my life ever any good? I'm desperately holding on, hoping to get through the weekend so I can go and see that Nut-doctor, and for what? I've got fuck all going on, apart from I think it's better to be breathing than not.

I'm delusional – that word is not going in any of our vocab sections – too harsh and black, none descriptive – worth mentioning but only to put it in its place. I must be delusional to think that writing all this down will help. My life was shit before the thoughts came so why am I hanging onto the hope that I can get through and make myself better? Not end up like Psycho Daren banged up in a hospital or prison? Because I want to get through to the end, finish writing this and hopefully be back walking the streets, stopping for coffee, very nice my dear, and could I have a nice piece of that carrot cake, you're a diamond... All the while I'm looking at the knife she's cutting it with and thinking, The blood splatter up the wall will be horrendous in here, but never mind, nice cake, and the bit I take will be the only one with no blood on it and as the scene unfolds, I'll turn to run, everything on freeze frame moving click by click, except I'm slightly faster than freeze-frame-click, one step at a time, the horror on everyone's face and a lad scrambling for the door, eyes bulging, knocking a table, falls over, beautiful height, and I let rip catching him with the boot, and up he goes, me moving slightly faster as his chops shake and his eyes roll, and I'm getting to giddy point by now as the staff run into each other not sure what the fuck's going on.

Come to think of it, this is probably why I've not been in a coffee shop for a while; too much steam and silver in there for my liking. That semi-colon there – first time I've ever used one, what do you think? Looks good, but makes me feel like I'm out of my depth. I'll have a ponder on that one. 'Ponder' now there's a word for you, relaxing, aimless, not hurried or edgy – that's in, no sweat. Aimless, you see, that's got me thinking about everything that has. Aimless is how this all started, how sweet a connection is that to have in the story? And here's why, These thoughts would drift by, aimless, like a balloon, when someone was close, or I wasn't occupied reading the paper, if someone was close, encroaching – I like 'encroaching', sounds like cockroach, which essentially is what I've become. A horrible cockroach scurrying about town. Black on the beautiful white, hurrying into little corners not sure what I'm doing or why.

I know we said we were going to try and not single out any of these posh words, but some of them I can't let go. How about we agree to cut back? That's sounds like a plan, and we can still be flexible – I like flexible, makes me feel fit and strong. Maybe we can slip flexible into the story for real to boost my image to the reader.

What was I saying there? Before the cockroach – oh yes, when people were too close like when you see a nice girl and you idly watch her going about her business thinking you could give her one, no trouble at all, yet the thoughts disappear as quick as they arrived. This is how these thoughts came about. The red balloon floating by while you are people watching through the steamy window of whatever café you go into to pass a few hours away, no harm.

Except mine feel like they aren't so harmless anymore. Like the balloon has been caught on something right in my vision and won't go away. I can't see past it, but I want to. I'm desperate to see past it, if I knew how I'd pop the fucking thing. That would be being violent, wouldn't it? No, I'd cut it loose, let it go and if it came back there'd be no problem because I'd know how to cut it loose again.

No worries there, I'd do whatever they told me to get to the bottom of this, except no one's told me. I blew it by not being honest with the Nut-doctor, and I realise that now. Sitting here, arm on this bench looking out into the dark, Old Storm on his way back down the bank after me, I wish I had some handcuffs, like that pro in The Warriors, because I'd cuff myself to this bench until someone came and took me back to the flat. Maybe V. She could be the one to find me. She should be my hero, because I was hers. In her time of need. Don't ask me how, but I helped her, brought her in, fed and clothed her, gave her a few smokes, and now – I've left her for dead.

I've just realised that she has no one. V doesn't have a soul, and the one person she'd turn to can't see his way to helping out. What have I done? Christmas in two days and I turf the poor fucker out into the dark to be kicked to shit by a load of Goths. Jesus Christ, what the hell has got into me? Have I no feeling left? A savage, is that what I've become? In this time when all I'm trying to do is get through the day?

I stood up and retched. The smell of whiskey shooting down my nose, and the stinking barman and bandit freak blowing through my thoughts, and where was V in all of this? God knows where, but this couldn't go on. I could throw myself off a bridge. What a horrible individual I've become with no value for human life. Am I right? Is that how you see this? I wish you could tell me, but you can't, because if you're reading this I never made it.

I marched into the dark, full of purpose, this wasn't over. I was being melo – melodramatic – nasty word, neither nothing nor something, like delusional, hard and black words, for a strained part of the story. I needed to get back on track, away from all this talk of not feeling too good. I needed to redeem myself and offer V a home for the night. Longer if she needed it.

12

I felt more elated than ever before when I came in front of the two generators at the side of the hospital. I looked down the street and it was beautiful. Cars covered in snow all looking the same shape. Bubble cars, thick white cars, that you could pick up and eat. Old Storm was some place else.

A nice choir, stepping out from behind the rumbling of the generators was what was needed to complete the scene. Just under the street lamp the choir are circling the lady at the front, all carrying their own lanterns and wearing Sally Army outfits with those hats that ruffle at the front like an old stage coach that Dick Turpin might hijack.

I walked up the road, turning full circle to look at the now peaceful Leazers Park. What a sight. This blanket of snow must have been some size because it had covered everything and wasn't stretched at all. You could put your hand in three foot deep across the whole town and make the best snowball of your life. It was getting colder, but there was no sign of frost, and only when Old Storm was on the rampage did it get difficult to move around. Not wanting to step out of this lovely scene, but needing to, I walked into the entrance of the hospital.

I've been here scores of times visiting dying relatives. Horrible place, but which hospital isn't? Who goes to a hospital and says, Hey what a laugh? We had a great time? I'll tell you who. Kids. Teenagers. They run riot in places like this. I once brought a friend in here. A real friend, not one of these work flakes you get lumbered with. He had a head injury. A wayward bottle landed on him in a bar, and I brought him up here and the place was like an army hospital during the war. Blood everywhere. Kids getting stitched up after fighting, but they weren't exactly grateful. They ran amok in the place, up and down the corridors on kids' toys with white sheets over their heads shouting this and that. It was funny, I'll give them that, but the staff must have been sick. We kept to ourselves, got him stitched up and got out.

I walked past the entrance and checked in the windows looking for V. The curtains were all drawn, no lights on. If I remember right, the bottom level windows were for outpatients, so V would probably be on a ward somewhere.

I kept getting closer to the door, then slipping away. Sniffing about like a stray, up to the doors, any movement inside, and I was away sniffing round lampposts and cocking my leg. What was I going to say? And then I thought, Why don't I just run in? Fast as I can, along the corridor and take cover somewhere until I figure out what to do.

The night porter came to the door and lit a cigarette. He was in one of those navy blue army jumpers with the patches on the elbows and shoulders, and that got me going proper. I mean, who is going to raid a hospital, people are trying to get out, for fuck's sakes? But then again, you've got all the drugs in there, haven't you? I get it now, and fuck me, opposite Leazers Park where all the smack heads are sleeping? He looked under-dressed now, with the day of the living dead scene taking place behind me. Michael Jackson and his good looking buddies stumbling out of the bushes.

The porter came over and asked if I was okay. I said I was just a bit up tight, you know, what with Christmas and everything and he knew what I meant. Plenty of people like me this time of year, he said, and that he felt that way himself at times. I quickly told him about V before I lost my bottle and bolted.

With him standing so close, things were getting strained. I was watching his feet. Black shoes, not that good a grip. We were in the car park and there were tracks where the ambulances had been and if I cracked him one he wouldn't stand a chance. And as he's getting up, that's when I'd freeze it, just then for a second, and boot, right in the face.

And then I started to fill up, my chest heaving, thinking want a terrible thought. This poor old man working night shift on shit wages, out here in the cold offering to help me and all I can think about is kicking him in the face. I tell you this is not nice and it's not going away. Soon as anyone comes near, I'm going to burst.

The porter put his arm around me and I wanted to yell out at him and say, Run, fuck off, do one mate, I'm not on the level, I'm not thinking straight! Take me to a room and lock the door until you can find someone who can help me out! But all I did was nod and watch his feet as he guided me into the hospital.

Once his feet were on solid ground, on the horsehair door mat, we were safe. I wasn't thinking about him slipping then, and on top of that, it was so bright it was like a fuck-off UFO had landed and I looked up and covered my face.

The porter went behind his desk and got his coffee mug. Blue, it was. Like a Blue Peter mug. And he asked me what I wanted and I said coffee and then I thought of Starbucks and all that silver and I changed my mind and asked for tea.

I started warming up and I didn't like it. I preferred to be out there and was thinking about making a run for it while I could before this up-standing pillar of the community made me an emotional wreck. The last thing I needed right now was someone being nice to me. I would fold and become a puddle on the floor.

Before he came back, I thought about V. The reason for being here. Never mind myself and worrying about fucking up. The one person I hadn't thought about doing in was V. Well, maybe a little, with the pizza knife, but I didn't, did I? If she's safe around me alone in the flat with a pizza knife, then she's safe, period. I like the word 'Period', you know. It's all American, isn't it? Only problem with having it in the final cut is that some fucker at work used it all the time. They're not going to win the league – period. So it'll have to go. Not unless I can forget about him and we can slip it in without me making a song and dance about it. We'll see.

Paddy the porter returned with a cup of tea and left me in the waiting area to drink it. When he returned I let it go about V. My good pal, but I can't remember her surname. What kind of a cunt am I? But he knew the score and didn't make any such assumptions. Judging by the amount of crumbs and hair on his jumper and niff coming of him, he knew what it was liked to be hemmed in. I might be jumping the gun, but I reckon he was a loner and this job suited him fine. Good for him. Getting settled in society, crumbs or no crumbs, he was making a go of it. I wish I knew his secret. I didn't know and was unlikely to find out by staring at his shoes, so I got it out about V and he knew exactly who she was and where I could find her.

Real quiet though, because he could lose his job for this. And you know what? I believed him. I think he would lose his job and let me tell you, him letting me in and trusting me got me going again. I couldn't give a fuck if the hospital ward I was sitting in collapsed, you wouldn't hear a peep out of me. Not me sir. I wouldn't let you down.

Shoulders back, off I went down the corridor. After a few steps I took my boots off because they were squeaking, and I didn't want that. Not for Paddy, who had just put his whole working life on the line for a complete stranger in a spot of bother. I came to V's ward and looked through the door.

13

Along the corridor was the ward desk, where I take it Matron sat stuffing her face and hoping no red lights came on. I couldn't see anyone, just the desk and some curtains to one of the rooms. This was V's ward alright. Paddy had said so, but he never said a room, and it got me thinking, would she be in with the rabble no matter what state she was in because she was a dosser? Or would she be treated like everyone else? You'd think everyone would be treat the same, but you never know.

I shuffled along the corridor carrying my boots, trying to get a look in but all the curtains were closed. As I got further along it was getting lighter and I could see someone behind the desk. Blue top, black hair, woman probably, she was sitting back, and my stomach was going. What was I doing here? Getting past Paddy was one thing but these people were razor sharp – family only, sir, oh you're her brother, what was her surname?

The nurse came out from behind the desk and as

she did, I moved against the wall and slowly turned the handle of the nearest door. I stepped inside, stifling a laugh. Honestly, the laughter was rising up and down my pipes like a strength hammer at the fairground. BING! BING!

I could hear footsteps and I went further into the dark and hid behind one of the curtains, holding my breath. On top of everything I was melting like a snowman, dripping all over the floor. If anyone came in here, they'd think someone had been out of bed and pissed all over. And they probably had, which meant I was wondering around in piss. Fuck me, what a scene. If ever there was One Flew Over the Cuckoo's Nest, this was it. Except I'd be right at home, playing cards with Randolf and the boys before they cut my brain out.

I hope nothing like that goes on. You know, if I turn myself in. I hope they don't think it's hereditary and start cutting lumps out of my brain. But then again, the way I'm up and down, I think I'd take the chance, but I wouldn't have a choice, would I?

Might not be so bad. Could be a decent place, nice people to talk to who are also fucked. Maybe not. Not for me. What? End up a dribbling wreck when I've done nothing wrong? Not for me. I'm going to see it through to Magic Monday. That's what this story is going to be called if I make it.

Magic Monday. That's when it's finished and I'm handing myself over to whatever and if telling you lot all about it isn't helping I'll stop that too. But for now, we're going to see V, see what these Goths have done.

14

On my way out the door I switched a couple of charts over on the beds and burst out laughing, falling out the door holding my mouth like I had just tasted a vindaloo. I staggered away from the desk and into the day room where the TV was and closed the door behind me and ran over to the window, opened it, and burst out laughing.

I got settled there, watching the snow again, looking down on the park and cars. Nothing happening. Calmed me right down. Then I thought about the man getting tablets shoved up his arse instead of down his throat and I was off again. Ridiculous and childish. I promised myself after seeing V I'd change them back, but the thought of it had me doubled over.

That's the thing in a hospital you have to laugh, don't you? You've got to make the most of what's happening because you're with fuck knows who, who will be snoring and farting and there's nothing you can do about it except fart back. Real stinkers, like my mate in bed five when the doctor slips one up tomorrow – Jesus that was bad, fuck me, that was terrible, you evil bastard. But funny, eh?

Just then the door opened and the nurse came in. She walked into the middle of the room and I didn't want to look at her, so I didn't. I stared out of the window and fidgeted with the rubber seal trying not to think about Mr X getting the wrong tablets.

She sounded okay, though. I wasn't really taking in what she was saying but it wasn't nasty, she wasn't throwing me out, then I felt her take my hand. She was inches from my face and steel flashed before my eyes and I backed away from her and very nearly brought my foot straight up the middle.

She said it was okay, that I wasn't to worry and everything was fine to see Veronica. I felt embarrassed and was nearly behind the sofa just keeping away from her. She said to follow her and she'd show me her room. She said V was on her own, and I'm thinking, result, V, a room in a warm hotel like this. At a cost obviously, but still, she might be able to string it out. I nearly said, Nursey, do you think she'll be able to string it out?

We passed the main desk, and I suddenly felt trapped, names on boards, gas masks and all sorts of shit. There was another nurse, smaller, all in white, smiling as we passed, but I was having none of it, stuck to the wall and a good few steps behind.

I stopped walking when she reached the door and opened it, arm outstretched saying V was in there, no rush, as long as I was quiet. The nurse walked off into the room opposite and I checked behind me and went in.

15

I closed the door behind me, but couldn't look at V for laughing. I couldn't. I had my head cocked to the side and walked over to the window, talking out the side of my mouth, letting this laugh out in little puffs, like the generators outside, puff, there you go, puff, out you get.

I couldn't hold the laugh in a second longer, so I grabbed the blanket off the bottom of V's bed, wrapped it over my head and dropped to my knees in the corner and let it go. I laughed my head off. Hard as I could I let it go until I was retching again. The whiff of whiskey brought back fond memories of having a swift one in the bar with bandit freak. Good times, it's what it's all about, isn't it? If you can't have a laugh and good time what the fuck's the point?

I sat up and wrapped the blanket around my neck and leant back against the wall, getting all calm again. I don't think I was laughing at V being in this bed. I couldn't think that because I would be hysterical. How bad would that be? Laughing at this? A disgrace, that's what.

I tell you what though, when I got bad news, like someone had died, I would smile. You ever had that? You know, when they say, Hey I'm sorry to tell you but your aunt has died, and you struggle to stop smirking. You know it's bad news and you don't find it funny, but fuck me what an effort not to laugh in the messenger's face. Well I reckon this is what's gone on here, because when I stepped through the door I knew I wasn't going to look at V, I just knew it. I felt like I was stepping of a fucking cliff when I came through that door.

When I got close to V's room it nearly sucked the life out of me. When I came through the door, all dramatic, something had to give, so now you know that, it doesn't look so bad. Sitting on the floor gives me a chance to get used to things.

I couldn't see V from where I was sitting. Just her clipboard. I should switch it with the next one along, see if she can get a few uppers and downers in her before they turf her out. Fuck me, what a place. What must V be thinking lying there? I turf her out and as soon as she shows any sign of recovery the hospital will sling her on the street with an A-Z telling her where the nearest soup kitchen is.

You ever been to a soup kitchen? Me neither,

but it can't be good, can it? V reckons it's not so bad. She said the worst sights were the old. Some of them not even homeless, just lonely and hungry, living in one bed suicide flats waiting to die. Fuck me, what a life.

That's what I mean, saving my life, for what? Look at these people on the streets fighting piles all their lives, being looked down on, losers like me saying, Well, I'm sure they'd be able to get a job in McDonalds. How many times have you seen a homeless person and thought, Poor fucker, God knows what tragedy got them into that doorway. Fucking never. Shame on all of us. I know some are smack heads, but not all. And who are we to judge?

We'll see how some cope. We'll see who's going to do what, the weak fuckers killing themselves because they can't stand the shame. Fuck that, I'm not weak. I'm not weak at all. Writing this down takes some doing, and telling you lot all about it takes balls – I love using the word 'balls' in that context. It's as American as 'period', but makes me laugh. He had balls of steel. Like it.

I stood up, took a look at V and was straight over to the window spewing that vile whiskey through my nose, tears running down my face. She had been done over properly and I couldn't take it. I felt so ashamed and I dropped to my knees next to her side and gently took hold of her hand.

Her face had been battered, and I was such a wimp, cowering down next to her hand not wanting to look up at the purple, swollen face, mouth open, at rest for a while. I held her hand, stroking down the fingers and wondering where V had been. Why had she ended up on the street, happy to talk to a stranger like me and feel comfortable to come back to my place for a bath and some food? And what would a good kicking like this do to her? Would she go back home? Did she have a home? If she did things mustn't be too good. No matter what your differences, nothing could be as bad as this.

I opened the window and cleaned the sick up off the window ledge, and thought, How dramatic have you become tonight? Talk about up and down, I hardly even know V and here I am rolling around the floor like her next of kin. Have a word.

And I did, but the light coming through the door set us in a scene. V and me, thrown together by Old Storm, our paths crossing and here we were indoors, side by side, and her hand was moving. My heart nearly stopped. Then she spoke. V started to speak and I didn't know what to do. I dashed to the door and pressed my face against the glass and checked Matron wasn't about, then went and sat next to her.

She didn't open her eyes, but I could hear her talking alright. She said my name. Tyler, is that you? I said, Who else? Like the saviour I was, and you know what – right there in a second she gave me everything I needed to get through to Monday. When I spoke, she smiled, ever so slightly, and I was more elated than I'd been all night and I wanted to tell her that, get everything out about bandit freak and the Blue Bell wine drinkers, but you know what? I never said anything. For once I thought about V and the night she was having and I squeezed her hand, nothing too hard, but she squeezed back and I could have opened that window and climbed up the drain pipe and onto the roof and called Old Storm over and got him onto the roof to dance with me. What a night! What a scene! Best scene of the night, and I never wanted it to end.

V asked if I was alright, and I said I was, you know, same as before, and I didn't know if she knew what that meant, because I didn't know if I'd said anything to her about how I was feeling.

She seemed happy with my answer, and then she pushed herself up and it felt like a huge wave had come over the top of the room and I needed to get out of the way of it. She sat up, eyes open and we were too close together, so I moved away and she asked for some water, which I got.

She said to sit back down, to take it easy, but her having her eyes open changed everything, and I needed to go. I opened the door and checked outside. There were two nurses talking, so I closed the door and came back inside. V slid down her pillow and closed her eyes, asking me to hold her hand. I waited a while then went over and sat in the chair and held her hand.

She never spoke. Which suited me, but it was hard not thinking about being in a room with a half naked women and it made me want to burst into tears having such a horrible thought. Then I got giddy, thinking, would she notice if I slipped my hand under the covers and had a rummage about? After that thought I got up and ran for it.

Past the nurses, down the stairs, Make way! Madman on the loose who wants to stick his hand under bed covers when the patient is asleep! I didn't even stop to say goodbye to Paddy, just stuck my hand up and ran out... and guess who was waiting?

Old Storm was full of power and purpose and I had to get my head down and shoulder into him to get one foot forward. I was giddy as hell, laughing as I went head to head with him. I was going into the park, the best place on earth and he wasn't going to stop me.

16

He threw me down the bank, and I was loving it! Snow up my nose, rolling and rolling, all the way down, and I was thinking, Go on get me in the lake you'll be doing me a favour, pal, stick me on the thin ice and let me flap about then cover me over.

I'd sink to the bottom, past all the syringes, which I'd stick into myself, one in the arm, one in the foot, deeper and deeper I would go, and here we are, passing another junkie, bandit freak's brother, isn't he handsome, not a single tooth in the top set, and I would kick him away, Get out of it you filthy bastard! You deserve to be here, but I don't.

Swim past, with the light cutting through, a sunken remote control boat, and the little boy standing at the side of the lake on a summer's day, and he's a little upset. Never mind old chap, pops will get you a new one before you've even got back to the car. In fact old bean, he's probably carrying three spare, and at a hundred a go, they're for nothing, so you won't mind me having this one. So

I pull the needles out of the car and swim through the weed and bamboo, all the while kicking bandit freak's brother off my tail. He knew I was destined for better things, this was a one-off, a temporary stop, Old Storm showing me what was coming if I didn't get myself sorted out, except he thought he was coming with me, getting out on the back of me like he had his whole life. Like thousands of people, all they do is watch others and get on the back of them.

If he can do it, why not me, bandit freak thinks. I'll just brown-nose up to him, Yes sir, no problem there, and the more brown-nosing the better they get at it until they become indispensable because they'll do anything they are told.

Brown-noser or not, I kick the fucker in the face, my first show of violence and I'm not proud of it, but you tell me how to get a bandit freak of your back when he's trying to bring you down to his level and he's stabbing away trying to get a needle through your jacket?

My head came out of the water and I opened my eyes and let the snow land on my tongue. I was at the bottom of the hill.

On further inspection I could see that I was in the middle of the footpath that went around the lake and Old Storm was rustling about in the bushes looking for someone.

Think what you like about this little episode but if you buy into nature being in charge, then when you need a helping hand, a cuff round the head, it gives it to you.

Old Storm hasn't left me on my own to dwell on things too much, and for that, I will be eternally grateful. 'Eternally grateful' is nice and peaceful, and ends things well. I hope to use it again, when I'm settled – just then the flat came into my mind and I could see everything a lot clearer. Things might not be so bad back there. Maybe I'm running from the one place I need to be. I've done my bit for V, it's late and the sooner I get to sleep, the sooner it's Saturday and only one more sleep and the quack will be open. Putting that into hours would be too much. What if I can't sleep? And what about the fucker below me? What if he plays his music? I wouldn't be happy about that.

I stood up, brushed most of the snow off and kept close to the bushes, not wanting to attract Old Storm. I looked towards the street, through the gap in the trees where the crossroads of footpaths came together next to the wooden bench.

I could see through to the main road and the shops, except there was a fuzziness about it now. Before the snowfall, it was clear, people moving about, the hot toddy couple waiting for a bus, except now it was Christmas card perfect, with no one in sight, and the fuzziness around it was like what you'd see below a lampshade. That was down to Old Storm, who had whipped up under the street lamps, windows, and even car door handles. He hadn't missed anything out, leaving only shapes of what was there before.

I followed the lake around, to the crossroads of footpaths, and in total awe, I walked into the finest scene of the night. I was entering the picture perfect high street, a slight buzz as I passed under some overhead cables, and into the middle of the road.

The traffic lights were a smudged amber and green, like one of those dot paintings by a famous artist, where a car is a yellow dot, lots of yellow dots, like all the cabs in New York. This scene had a white film over it and then the colours and I was walking across the canvas. I'd never felt anything like it before.

I looked back at Leazers Park, at peace with itself, but also miffed, arms folded, upset that I had moved on to bigger and better things. I had myself a little dance, a quick shuffle, all Frank Sinatra, grabbing the lamppost and swinging around.

I had another look back at Leazers, who was huffing and puffing – and that was it exactly. The hospital and lake and park and the Black Bull were a force to be reckoned with. Over here the fighting was finished, resistance gone, and it was majestic. Majestic will be in the final cut and the cover of this story will be this scene.

17

I was on my way to the flat when I spotted a light
on and a puff of smoke. I crossed over the road.
Who would stay open tonight? When I got closer I
saw it was one of those café bars where you can
have a cappuccino or a cocktail.

I looked through the window, over the snow and
under the steam, and it was all American with big
red booths. I tell you, I've never wanted to go in a
place more in my life and order some eggs sunny
side up like they do on TV. I looked around and
thought, One drink, something to eat, then home.

I half opened the door, just to have a look. It
could have been full of people for all I knew, but
the scene I had in my mind was the waiter behind
the bar and just me. Him washing up, casually
watching a portable TV next to the sink, not
bothered about doing night shift because he had
done it for so long. That's what I had in mind, all
the time in the world, no one around.

I pushed the door open and poked my head in,

like I was looking in a broom cupboard with no light on – quick scan up and down. All clear. Not even the waiter, and it wasn't all bright, like the hospital. I walked in and felt right at home.

I loosened off, like I did at the Black Bull, and this looked good – not a soul. Who would be out at this time of night? Apart from idiots and loners like me, but even then they would have to be from the city, wouldn't they? Just ask the hot toddy couple about transportation tonight. And I thought about them as I walked along past the booths, crouched over slightly, you know, like off one of those horror films where the whole world is dead apart from a couple of survivors and you stumble upon a sign of life.

I got to the end of the counter which was gleaming silver. I looked away and slipped into a booth. Right in I was. Not even next to the door. I felt excited not stopping at the entrance, but I couldn't because I wanted to see the two hot toddy snowmen at the bust stop, him with his frozen hand sticking out. What a scene. But they weren't there, probably picked up on CCTV and taken to V's ward.

There was a radio on, and I felt relaxed enough to take my coat off. As soon as I laid it down next to me, I got to thinking, what would I do if a crowd came in and they sat either side of me, shouting, messing around, and all this silver and shit?

I got to the door, turned and looked at the place. You won't believe it but it really was all American, like 'period' and 'balls' and all it needed was a juke box and the booths looked so good and warm, like on the films when people meet up for breakfast over a strong coffee and pass a gun under the table. This was the place, plonked just along from the flat and all this time I never knew about it.

I opened the door to leave and Old Storm was racing down the middle of the street looking for me, so I shut it again, then I heard a voice. It was the waitress behind the counter.

She was wearing a vest and had a purple Mohican. What a fucking haircut. It was purple, but not gelled or anything just loosely wafting about. Light purple and it looked unbelievable. I'd never seen anything like it.

She took a draw on her cigarette, placed it back in the ashtray and walked forward to the counter. She smiled and said she hoped I didn't mind that she was smoking indoors, it was too cold out, and she hadn't had a customer in hours. I nodded, hand still on the door handle. I looked down at my feet, all soaking and melting and I was going to bolt, best thing I could think off, her standing there in a vest, purple Mohican, smoking, and all that silver.

I couldn't be on with it, and in any case, I was only going to have one drink and go back to the flat and be done with it until tomorrow.

I promised myself that I would come back one night, when I felt okay, and I would sit and chat with the waitress, all casual, and keep her company, maybe even bring V here a couple of times a week, a regular thing, and the three of us could share a booth. That would be nice and them two could do most of the talking, and I'd just chip in with the odd word, nothing heavy, and they wouldn't get sick of me or start bitching about me when I went to the toilet, and because we only came one or twice a week we wouldn't get sick of each other.

I was thinking all this and feeling pretty good about it when she took hold of my arm and led me to a booth. She said something about that one being free, and joked that I was lucky to get a seat.

She went back behind the counter and started messing about. Steam blasting in the air, and it made me feel warm so I took my coat off. Struggled out of the thing and flung it on the opposite side, leaving me with plenty of space. I ran my hand through my hair and took my scarf off. I didn't feel at all relaxed, but she wasn't paying me any attention, which was good.

Not wanting to be around people, but needing to

be, is a hard one to figure out, not unless you're around nature. That's okay because nature's face is so big you don't know how close you are to it, unlike this punk rock chick who has decided to come and take my order. You want to hear it? Here you go,

'Right, then, what can I get you?'

'A coffee and I'll have something to eat.'

'I can do you breakfast if you want? Not meant to until eight, but if that's what you want, you can have it.' She stepped up into the booth, leant across and pointed at my menu. 'This is what you want to try it'll keep you going all night. I had one and never ate for two days.'

She smirked at that and so did I. I said, Okay, stick me down for one of them, but be it on your shoulders, and I think she smirked again, but couldn't be sure. I hoped I said it in a funny way and not leery, because I felt leery, even though I wasn't even directly looking at her, sort of nodding and speaking straight ahead – I didn't want to look at her.

She came back over with my coffee and said I could have as many refills as I wanted, no cost, and then she slid across to the other side of the booth and I clenched my legs together, tight at the knee caps, and I was frozen. Then I looked at her.

I wanted to say something, but I had nothing.

Just the sound of my heart hammering. All I could think of was a big red dot pounding hard, but slow, boom, boom, boom.

She seemed alright with things and I was enjoying the company, it was good, and we were separated by the booth, then she pulled out her smokes and offered me one, and I said no, have one of mine and I was fumbling around pulling my coat over the table from the other side and it lashed her in the face, but she just laughed, so I laughed, and got them out, and I said I wasn't feeling my best tonight and sort of lifted my hands up, it was the least I could do and I was still looking at her and not thinking about caving her head in, and let me tell you the second look with no bad thoughts, and I was on my way, a right old chatter-box I was, and I nearly got on about Old Storm, but she beat me to it and told me how bad it was working here.

'Minimum wage, late nights and you make fuck all in tips.' My face must have dropped, and she said, 'No offence! Not you, you seem nice, manners, unlike some of them that come in here. And I'm staying in the hostel round the corner, ten to a room. Not the greatest gig I've ever had.'

She went on like this, and we had a few smokes, drank a coffee, and she got me the breakfast sandwich, but I wasn't hungry, so she picked at it, and so did I, just the bacon and sausage, and then my phone bleeped.

I looked at it and it was a text – top gear, any chance tonight? Sixes.

I was laughing, not daft, just chuckling at him calling himself Sixes, when the punk rock chick came over my shoulder and read the text. She slipped into the other side of the booth, and I thought, shouldn't be reading other people's texts, breakfast-share or no breakfast-share, and things changed from then.

Rock chick went on about how she had taken this gear and that gear, and how she loved getting out of it, then she asked me if I had any freebies I needed testing out, and that was when she became too close and I needed to get out.

I grabbed my coat, and she said suit yourself, and I could have smashed her head into the table and thrown her behind the counter into all the silver and steam, but I was too quick for myself and I ran for the door and I thought, You're not fit to lace V's boots, and I was off down the road, thinking about Sixes and whether or not to off-load all the gear now and be done with it.

18

I slowly opened the door to the flat, expecting someone to be there. I thought after the police were watching the place, they might have an ambush ready for me.

I stood at the bottom of the stairs, in the dark, listening. I could hear the fan in the bathroom. It hadn't been switched on, but the wind was spinning it around. That's all I could hear, but I still didn't want to switch the light on.

I took my jacket off, thinking that maybe someone had heard about the deals going down with Sixes and the other Goths and they were tooled up ready to roll me.

The lad I get the gear off is all the best of friends with me, just like I was with Sixes, and just like I couldn't give a shit about Sixes, this lad could easily set me up to be rolled in my own flat. He'd know where I lived, me being a regular. So he could be upstairs waiting.

Unlike Sixes, I know this fucker doesn't give a

shit about me. As long as I get my gear to flog every week, why should we be anything but business associates?

When I was ordering a 9-bar of dope, I was safe. Who would come and do you for a 9-bar? No one, not worth it. And don't forget this place is like Fort Knox, so getting in isn't a stroll, but there again, you've got that idiot down stairs who would happily let someone drill through his living room ceiling for a fiver. Scum bag. Never worked a day in his life and he has three kids and the mother's out all day working while he bets on the horses. How typical is that?

You can see why I didn't want to come back. It's hardly a tranquil place to get your head down and pull yourself together. Especially with so much gear on the premises.

I walked up the stairs, stopping halfway and listening. The fan in the bathroom was still whizzing round, Old Storm would be making sure of that, and just then, an image of the flat came into my mind. It was a view from the other side of the road and I was desperate to look out the window and see if it really looked so perfect.

Old Storm wouldn't be leaving me tonight. Wherever I have gone the one thing helping me out by both being there and not, is Old Storm, and just because I was back at the flat, it didn't mean he would be leaving me.

I had a vision of him outside, after whipping round the kid's park and the tower blocks, he would cover my flat from top to bottom, make it as peaceful looking as the diner in town, before hanging his hat up somewhere close by, ready for me to come out. You watch, if I go out again tonight, he'll come from nowhere and keep me company.

At the top of the stairs I decided to go for it and see what was going on, so I switched both the kitchen and living room lights on, darted into the kitchen and picked the bread knife up.

Into bedroom one – everything sweet, and bedroom two – still full of shit, bathroom – clear, and back into the kitchen. I knelt down, pulled the floorboards up and stuck my hand in and started bringing the gear out. There was a 9-bar, coke, ketamine, acid, and Es. I sat back, feeling all queasy. I looked up, squinting at the dim light. Is this what it had come to? Is this who I am now? Early in the morning, sitting in a flat on the wet floor with a grands worth of drugs in front of me?

I often wondered what I would be doing when my number was called. And let me tell you, you're forgotten quicker than by the cunts you worked with. They wouldn't even come to your funeral.

What's the point? He's dead now? It's not going to do him any good. Fucking scum.

And if it was my time now, like in three seconds, if I stretched up and got the knife and stabbed it into my neck, can you imagine the stories floating about when someone found me? Who would find me? Apart from V, and I don't think she has a key. Who would save me?

Fucking no one. Stories about a double life as a drug dealer killed in a turf war, or worse, killed myself because I couldn't take it. This is it right here, the reason I'm seeing this through to Monday. I've seen the fuckers who got this mess started. To kill yourself is the lowest way out. Lowest of the low. I'd rather be in with the numb heads trying to figure this out, because it can be figured out. Surely the authorities will see that, and if they read this, then I've come clean properly and maybe they've seen this a hundred times over and can say, Tyler, don't worry, these nasty thoughts happen to everyone, yours have just floated to the surface, all we need to do is weigh them down.

Well, I'm up for giving it a fight, because I won't be like those leeches in the banks. Like that multi-millionaire parasite the other day who hung himself, leaving the kids and wife to deal with everything, just because his shares or some shit had gone down the pan. He had probably kissed arse his whole life, but when it came to the crunch and his work buddies had disappeared up someone else's backside, he didn't have an ounce of decency in him to fight on. What a fucking scene. Worst of the night. I knew I shouldn't have come back. There is nowhere to escape to in here. I can't run off with Old Storm, I can't do anything but face myself. And I can't do it. Not right now. Not until I've seen that Nut-doctor, but where is he now?

I went into my bedroom, and there, on my bedside table, was his card.

19

I came back in and switched the lamp and TV on. Volume right down, all nice and cosy. Some Christmas shit was on. Probably a Christmas Carol, but I wasn't interested. I had a plan.

I started clearing the table, ashtrays, papers and bills. You've never seen so many. I didn't even know half of these had come, and I started thinking that maybe V had opened some of my mail when she had been staying here and hid it under the papers. Not out of nastiness, just to protect me from them, because you can see a red bill a mile off. Danger! Run for cover we're going to take you down! We don't care how many charities you give to or who you know is dying! Screams out at you when it hits the mat, and they'd rather break you and send you under than hear reason and take a part payment.

Sneaky old V the dosser. She was only thinking of me, which is understandable, so I won't be holding anything against her, and in any case, there isn't a whole lot I could do about it no matter how many reds came. I stopped trying to stack the numbers a long time back.

After clearing the table I went into the kitchen and got a damp cloth, a tea towel and the bread knife. I had no immediate use for the knife, but I just couldn't leave it lying there on its own. It was like a sword, a shining light. It had entered my thoughts so many times today that it felt like it belonged in my hand. I needed it with me, and not just haphazardly thrown across the bench, so I picked it up and brought it into the living room.

I wiped the coffee table down and got a feeling that there was someone behind me and spun around. I know this sounds all creepy, but being in a flat alone, especially mine, can do this to you. The landing light is fucked so you're always looking into the dark and can just see the outline of the white banister, or the frame of the bedroom door, dependent on what is flashing from the TV, and you can never be sure if anyone is there. Another good reason for the extreme security, which, incidentally, I've left open. If Old Storm wants to come in, he's more than welcome.

Like a surgeon, I laid out my tools to get me through the next hour. If all else failed, I'd go back and stay with V. The safest place for now, and she wouldn't mind at all. In fact, she's probably up out of bed, loping around like some hunchback looking for me on the ward. So yeah, I'll be heading in to see her. I wouldn't mind being in better fettle, though. You know, like on the mend, rather than like this, because I think she was frightened in here last time, she sort of kept away from me, which is not like her.

On the table then, the kitchen knife, TV remote, all the drugs, evenly spaced out so I can get some deals bagged up, my mobile and Nut-job's card. His card is the thing that has me up-beat. So, two things. We need to know if Sixes knows anything about the attack on V and if Nut-job does night visits. I dialled his number.

20

I hung up as soon as he answered and went walk
about round the flat, mad as The March Hare.
Whoopee! I'm a nutter, doctor, and I'm so
desperate tonight, and no I'm not under the
influence, but I feel the need to ring you and get
you and your good wife to take off your eye
patches and jump up out of bed so I can tell you
I'm not feeling too good. Tell you that I'm afraid
and my only friend is Old Storm, but also that I'm
not really off my rocker, just a little mixed up and
I need you to reassure me that I won't be dragged
away to have a lump cut out of my brain. This is the
thing, doctor, I'm trusting you here, client
confidentiality, but you've got a duty to the state
and to me, haven't you?

I had a sweat on and I was off it. I'd just called a
complete stranger and hung up. What the fuck does
he expect giving his number out to patients? He
must get loads of calls, and he never mentioned
anything to me about not ringing if it was an

emergency. In fact, he said next to nothing, period. I think it was more his fault than mine, because I'm willing to let go a little, up to a point. I know I need help. If I know I need help and had the guts to go and see him, then surely it's up to Nut-job to handle me properly, isn't it? To get the information out of me and guide me through the weekend and set up other appointments? I know I kept stuff from him, but he must have known that. I'm trawling back through the day finding out just who has done me a wrong turn, and believe me, there are many, not least of all Nut-job.

Have I got no one else to turn to? Friends, family, mother, father, brother, uncles, aunts, I've got them all, but how the fuck do you go to your mother and say, Look, this is going to sound a bit off, but I have a burning desire to boot you in the face, and that goes double for pops? You alright with that, mother? It's no big deal, but take my advice and don't bend down to get those scones out the oven, because banjo, right in the chops, and God knows what happens if I actually carry it out. So mother, what's your advice? Mother? At this point all doors would be locked and the ambulance and white coats would be on their way and my mother would be running through the house shouting, Mayday! Mayday! We have a live one aboard the vessel!

My family, for my own good, would be first to turn me in and I wouldn't blame them. If I can get things mended behind closed doors, all the better, because once I cross over and make this public knowledge, I'm finished. Job, family, the couple of mates I have left – fucked.

I looked at his card again and shook my head. What could he do at this time of night anyway? And if I was that desperate, why not ring my family? I got a shiver at that thought and stuck the card in my pocket.

Ringing home was out of the question. The shame of it all. No job, a drug dealer, nutter, I might as well become a mass murderer and be done with it. Be one of these people that go back to their place of work, all pissed off at getting the elbow and open fire, paper flitting into the air as I shoot up the photocopier, people running for cover that I don't even know. So boring though, isn't it? Who wants ten seconds of fame? Not me. I just want to get back with you lot.

My phone bleeped again and it was Sixes. Nice one m8 on me way. I deleted it and went into the kitchen. I flicked the kettle on and leaned against the counter thinking of V. What a shift she must have put in tonight. Her face was a right mess. She looked like she had been fished out of the river, all bloated and purple. Horrible sight, and to think someone would be lying in bed now not giving a shit that they had hospitalised another human being. All I knew from the information I had gathered was that it was Goths. Definitely Goths, but there are so many of them, and they all hang out down the park, so there's no way of knowing who had done what unless you could get them talking, and I wasn't in a chatty mood.

The kettle boiled and I poured the water into my cup, added milk to the coffee and walked towards the settee. I got an image of V sitting on the chair there chatting away like she had earlier, and I could see her damp hair hanging over her cheek and I remember thinking she didn't look so old and she had lovely clean teeth, real bobby dazzlers, and as I came behind her, the cup of coffee was becoming harder and harder to keep a hold of and I just wanted to swill her with it, right in the face. I quickly got past the chair and put the coffee down.

I remember having that feeling when I was in a café not so long back. I walked past a table of people and someone stood up, inches from my face, and I thought, I could swill you right now, this second. And I had to get away quick sharp. I thought nothing of it, and got myself a nice seat out of the way and kept my head down. All the chat going on above my head and I kept blowing on my coffee, thinking, he nearly got it.

When I walked outside, I remember looking around, all clear headed, thinking, where am I going? Like I'd forgot why I was there. I started walking away down the street, frowning, until I remembered I'd come into town for a magazine. That was it, the big realisation that I was after a magazine, and off I went, all happy that I was back on the ball.

I sipped the coffee and had a good look at the gear. Sixes was after three grammes of toot. I've not touched the stuff before. According to Psycho Daren it's a real head buster, gets them sky high and they can never get enough down them when they're partying. That's why he said to double up on the order. Drip feed them and they'll pay a fortune for it.

Toot was the posh-boy's drug, so Sixes pitching in with an initial three gramme order meant he was a posh Goth and not some pissed-up dope head that would boot a dosser in the face. That was him out of the frame for now, but he could still be a good source of information.

I knocked three one gramme wraps up and a two gramme wrap. I also put ten E into a bag, then I suddenly felt sick to the stomach looking at all this shit.

What the hell was I doing here? Is this what I'd become? And right there I felt the worst I'd felt all night. I was in trouble, sure enough, but this was my response? Deep down when I was battling and fighting something, I had turned to this. Ripping people of their sanity and pumping them full of shit I knew nothing about. What kind of normal kid does this, no matter what trouble they are in?

And it's not like I can turn around and say, I've tested it and you're safe with that, boys. I'm punting them anything, playing on their addictions and even trying to throw a few E in to get them properly fucked.

Fucking lowlife existence this, and I'm not being a part of it. This is crossing the line right here. I don't need to become this. It's the last money I have in the world, but do I want my happiness back at the expense of some skinny young Goths who are none the wiser?

A few deals of dope which I smoke myself are fine, but this is disgusting, and I'm close to tears. Is this what's at the core of me? Do to others what has been done to you?

Deep down I thought if they got to the bottom of this they would say, There was never ever a chance that Tyler would have stepped over – no one has ever been in danger, only himself, and the fighting spirit of the man is there to be seen and must be admired.

I washed every last bit of toot down the sink and it felt good. The whole fucking lot, out of circulation, not up anyone's nose. The ketamine next – whatever that shit was it wasn't getting distributed by me.

Fuck everything and everyone else. You think I owe Sixes anything? Fuck Sixes, I've done him a favour, and I moved around the flat, like a ballroom dancer, cha, cha, cha, picking the rest of the gear up as I went, and down the sink, there you go, all nicely done, making things even with the Gods, Why sir, we knew this would happen all along, you're a diamond in the rough.

And so it went on, cha, cha, cha, sliding between the sofa and TV, cha, cha, cha, and back to the sink, and down you go, dancing all light and airy nothing to hold me back, I'm coming through.

Like a breeze, I was back at the sink with only the bread knife left to go. I wanted to keep it close by, so I twirled around, all Fancy Dan, and slipped it down the back of my jeans, nice and snug, to protect me from all that care, and to protect me from myself...

Down with that coffee Tyler, because believe me I will cut your hand off and then you won't be able to hurt, scald or boot anyone. And I was in total agreement, and couldn't have been happier, a spring in my stride, but we had no room to dance, so on with my jacket, cha cha cha, and down the stairs, and there he was over in the park, dancing around waiting for me. A quick whistle and he was behind me and we took off down the street like a whirl wind, arms outstretched to the side, a bird and a plane, past doorways, down streets, across traffic signals and along footpaths, whooshing this way and that, no wild life, no life at all, just me and Old Storm free of inhibitions, free of it all, and on I went, running and skidding, like I was being chased, an old black and white film at Christmas time. That was the scene as I skidded to a corner, all Oliver Twist, and ran after the Artful Dodger, in here, in here, and on I went, along an alley, over a car, nothing stopping us as we ran from the policeman, the slow moving plod that wanted to take us to the pen.

We kept running, The Dodger and me, and every corner was a sharp turn, then we dashed across the open square, Old Storm nearly taking us down the street, What a scene! What a scene! We were free, free from it all and the police, a black shadow way behind us, not knowing where to go or what to do. Nothing could stop us as we let Old Storm take us, dashing into doorways, grabbing what we could, Hey, come back here!

Everything peeling off us as we got sucked further and further in. What a scene! Best scene of the night, never have I felt like this, so light I could take off and fly across rooftops, hopping from house to house, across the whole world, nothing could stop me.

A life like a butterfly, part of nature was where I needed to be and I was on my way and would stay with Old Storm as long as he would have me, and so it went on, and as we landed in the square where beggars and fruit stalls would be during the day, we danced, cha, cha, cha, around the seats, Yes my lord, not this evening, not for me, and then I pinched some food of his plate, and off we went, the force of Old Storm behind lifting me into the night, through the park, over the junkies and up to V.

Flying past V's window, I could have landed on the roof and hung over like a bat, and given her a knock but I was her friend and didn't want to disturb her, so off we went, on and on, through the town, across playing fields, no one around, just Old Storm and me, and so it went on, the night so young and fresh, like us, with no cares in the world, a life ahead of us, we need never see anyone again, never stopping for longer than a second to wish someone good day and grab an apple, and then we'd be away, the Artful Dodger and me, always one step ahead...

21

I woke up on the settee. The light was coming through the curtains, which were pulled to one side. Why didn't I shut them last night? Last night. I was so tired that I crawled up the stairs and flung myself at the settee. That's what happened, and the night is now gone and I'm still here and no one is hurt.

I sat up and tried to pull myself together. It wasn't going to be easy, not after a night like that, and it was giving me a headache trying to think of everything that had happened and I could only think back as far as running with the Artful Dodger, burning off some energy to try to get to sleep, and that's all I wanted to remember.

I lit up and took a big draw, then fell back over. I blew smoke rings and watched the cigarette burn down, like a firecracker with no sound, absolute waste. No sell-on value, just polluting the air and my lungs. The first of the day getting me light-headed and I was pleased with the feeling because my head felt like it had been in a vice. Not a vice, that's shit, when was the last time any of us saw a vice? Let's say my head had been trapped in a lift door, like The Shining. You can't get any more appropriate than that the way I've been feeling, can you?

Good description that and I would love to see them in the office now if I kept my face there, letting the doors whack of it until I dropped to my knees. Then I would lie there splattered with blood, my head to one side, the doors opening and closing, BANG! Yes two sugars thanks, BANG! Who's in the bran tub? BANG! What is that awful stench coming from the lifts we'll have to get it cleared up it will kill the ambience at the Christmas party tonight and we can't have that, BANG! Mistletoe anyone?

I know the fucker that would be mincing about doing all the talking and he'd get it first. He's petrified of me. Every time there was a work do he kept out of my way. Mind you, so did most of the others. They couldn't wait until I was out of the way, and I remember the outbursts of laughing, and that broke my dream – I was in an old pub with a bandit and I couldn't stop laughing.

This laughing out loud I've done for as far back as I can remember, even when I was feeling okay. It's a defence mechanism, you see. When there were three sets of feet hanging out the bosses' arse, I laughed out loud deliberately, letting The Click know I knew I was being excluded. Ha-fucking-ha, get that down you, so they must have been used to it by the time I was thinking of volleying them in the face and going into one proper.

I tell you what really sets me off, when you're not as pissed as everyone else and someone has lost it and they're sucking up to the boss – what a laugh. When I spot it, I move in for the kill getting as close I can, moving from group to group, who are all happy to get shot of me, fucking weirdo, and I get up real close, and then start whispering in the person's ear if the boss turns away. Stuff like, if it's a woman – just drop to your knees, no one is looking, or if it's a lad – stick your hand down the back of his pants and have a sample, and I tell you I'm hysterical, that's what sets me away, but amazing as it is, the same person will be sucking up again within ten minutes guaranteed because they're so pissed on trebles they can't remember. Fucking marvellous.

I went into the kitchen and flicked the kettle on. Why, I don't know, because drinking tea and coffee isn't exactly refreshing. It's just habit, but I needed to keep the habit going because my head was pounding. I felt sick and ran into the bathroom and up it came, again and again, and my head was getting tighter and I flopped onto the floor, all limp. I could smell whiskey and then I remembered that bar from last night, and the not knowing what else happened last night had my head whirling so I crawled over to the sink and was sick some more, right from the pit of my stinking gut. I felt terrible, then I got a sharp pain in my back. I felt the bottom of my back and pulled out the kitchen knife.

I ran the knife across the palm of my hand. Gentle and firm, along the life-line or whatever those crank fortune tellers call it. I watched the line go red and the blood come out, light red, not dark, so it wasn't deep. It was good to watch and I felt like I deserved it.

I squeezed my hand shut and then opened it and it had smudged, making the line thicker as blood continued to pour out. I stood up, trying to steady myself, but my foot slipped on a magazine on the floor. I picked it up. It was The Big Issue. I never buy it so it must be V's. It was turned over to the missing person's page and there was a picture of V and I went all funny and had to grab the sink, like I didn't know what was happening.

I quickly washed my hand and wrapped some toilet paper around it and came into the living room and sat down.

So V was in The Big Issue the sly fucker. Not a

word to me and she's staying in my pad. I think I'm entitled to an explanation, don't you? When it becomes public knowledge, the very least you can expect is that your friends keep you up to speed. It's like being in the office, always the last to know. The world's fucked, don't matter where you are, every fucker is keeping it from you. No one is straight with you. You've always got to keep your guard up, and then when you offer an olive branch – bang! Another revelation and embarrassment.

V of all people, after everything we've been through, and last night is rushing back, the hospital, I was in there, keeping an eye on her, and this is the thanks I get, fucking secrecy when she's in trouble. I'm not good enough to know. Well fuck her. She's out. I'm back on my own.

I launched the magazine across the room. As I did, the doorbell went. It best not be V, not after this last carry-on.

I stood at the window looking down and I couldn't see who it was, so I moved to the side and looked from the best angle I could. Ring, ring. Ring, ring. Impatient fucker, but who are you?

Then he stood back and looked up and I fell back over, holding my mouth, I couldn't believe it. It was only Richard from work.

22

Let me tell you about Richard. He's taller than me, say six foot for argument's sake, and he's got tipped blonde hair. Tipped hair, proper Nancy Boy, but not gay I don't think. He's not all hands and feminine or anything, more a smooth operator, who likes to be everyone's best pal. Girls, bosses, lowlifes, all get on with Richard. Yet when I first started, he was the one to blank me for a good few days. Like it would take a great deal of effort to gain his respect and trust. By the end of the week, when I hadn't given the pink shirt wearing cunt the time of day, he was over asking me about this and that, trying to get all personal, letting me know The Gang were going down the bar after work if I fancied a swifty. A swifty, as if that was all street and would get him on my level.

Richard is the kid in the office who reckons he can switch-hit and be street in every situation and every click. He reckons he can move around the room, taking the best out of every conversation, being the main man with the punch line. Richard hasn't got an identity, he's a walking fucking cliché and he's ended up at my front door in the snow. He can only be here for one thing and that's his phone. Someone had grassed me up for nicking it and now switch-hitter was here to collect.

The doorbell went again as I came across the living room and into the kitchen. I went under the sink for a bucket and noticed the hatch open where the stash was, and thought I'd check that later. I rifled around the top cupboard through my spices, looking for anything to put in the water. I was hoping for food dye, but I don't think there was any, so while the bucket filled up I shook everything I could get my hands on into it. Chilli seeds, cumin, gravy granules, nothing a problem for you Richy.

I got the bucket and walked across the living room. The picture of V in the magazine caught my eye and I went all funny again. I could see her upside down, long hair like a student, smiling, and I thought, Give her chance for Christ sake's, she's had a rough trot, she was probably going to tell you when she got a chance. She would have been nervous and couldn't come straight out and tell me, and God knows she's had her chances, but I suppose with her having the magazine out and being all comfortable in here, she thought she couldn't tell me about it, in case it upset the way things were.

I put the bucket down and walked over to the magazine and I felt more shamed than ever before in my life. I felt like I had judged her before I'd even heard her story. I only knew the V that slept in doorways, and because I had never asked, the life she had before didn't exist.

V had been missing for two years. Those words hit me right in the middle of the chest. I thought of her legs tucked beneath her on hard concrete for two years. Month after month and she'd survived, and now this.

Well, her luck was about to change because I was going to go up and get her from the hospital and sort her out. Put her right. Help her and help myself. This is what's wrong with the world right now. Nothing's at face value. What you think you see, isn't real. What's real is hidden behind the masks of back-stabbers and conmen, and that's how we've all ended up like this.

Did I ask V about her past? Unspoken rule, we always chatted about the here and now. That was our way and how we had became so close, and all along she had a past that needed unearthing, and now it was hot on her tail and she didn't know what to do about it.

I read on and it said she was twenty-seven, which

is about right when she's scrubbed up, and that she was missing from the Harrogate area. Harrogate, excuse me, she's a toff. Bit of a come-down, but then again, society does that to you no matter where you pitch in from. I read on and it said that her disappearance was out of character. There was a number to ring, but I wouldn't even dream of it. It would be like V ringing my family – unforgivable.

I put the magazine down, and I noticed some white powder on the table and I got a spaced out feeling, like someone had been in the flat, then I remembered under the sink, the floor board up, and last night came back to me, getting shot of the toot, and I felt all potty again, that I'd done away with all that gear, what was I thinking of?! Honestly, I can barely keep track of myself. I tell you these whims just take you away like a gust of wind, and I love the feeling of being taken away from myself.

I balanced the bucket on the windowsill and opened the window. It was the big window, the emergency exit apparently. This was the one you flung yourself out of onto the public pavement and broke your legs when there was a chip pan fire. I looked down and Richard had gone.

The snow was coming down steadily and across the road the gritters were out. They couldn't do much and there wasn't a single car on the move, just people hurrying around, chins tucked into their chests.

A few lads were having a snowball fight and they were coming down the road and I knew if any of them came under my window it would be too much and I needed to come inside. It was cold and my knuckles were white from gripping the bucket handle, and I needed to come in and pour the bucket of shit down the sink, but I couldn't move, feeling all mad again as the lads ran across the road, one side to the other, scrumming each other with snow, and my stomach was going, and they were nearly underneath my window, and I'm thinking, Get yourself inside and shut the window! But I couldn't help myself and as fate would have it they stopped under my window and I've never felt a buzz like it as I held onto the handle. Then I tipped the whole lot onto them, brown sludge stotting off their hats and onto the snow. I snapped the window shut and dropped down, biting my knuckles, absolutely hysterical.

I crawled along the floor, past the coffee table and behind the armchair and lay on my back and laughed as loud as I had laughed in my life. It got worse when I thought of the two lads leaning against the downstairs wall, taking a breather, watching their mates, then sloosh! On your head, son! What a beauty! Random kids swilled with everything out of my kitchen. Fucking hilarious or what?

You don't get better than that for entertainment. I got thinking about the weather and all that shit on them, and the two lad's faces just before they realised what had happened. That moment of complete and utter astonishment, the eyes opening, and freeze! Hold it there, that's the deal right there, the look on their faces. And think about the justice. Those scumbags would have been causing havoc all day. The snow was the sweetest I'd ever seen for making snow balls, and they were off school running riot, so no doubt cars and pensioners and other kids would have been getting it both barrels from these, so this was pay back. It happened so fast, they'll never really know if it was meant for them, bad luck, or what.

Just then, the front window crashed through and I dived onto the floor and crawled behind the chair and all I could hear were voices, and wind, and I thought about Old Storm last night, and I felt elated again, and I stood up and in he came forcing the curtains back, and I opened my arms, Where have you been?

And back it came, floating into my mind, the fun we'd been having in the park, and the hot toddy couple and Old Storm blowing me around. That was welcoming relief and here he was in broad daylight, by hook or crook, in my flat, wafting the curtains and bringing a chill to the place.

I didn't want to be rude, but when I thought about it, he couldn't come in. All the electrical stuff would get damaged. Then I thought, well throw them out, you won't be here after tomorrow anyway, but then I might be because I don't have any gear to sell to get a plane ticket. And then I started to feel sick and I knew it was because too much information was rushing through my head. I needed to be outside, feeling that fresh air and snow, but what about all the people outside? The whole town would be out during the day and it would be like The Blue Bell, full of them, and I couldn't be on with that today. Not today.

I opened the curtains and the kids had gone. When that window broke they would have hit the turbo, and they'll be happy that they've evened the score.

Settling a score is a way to get things off your chest. Get things going again, and I'm thinking that's what I need to do, but what I need to do first is go see that lady that is now sprawled across my coffee table in that magazine, because tonight could be too late. She's hardly going to go back to the same doorway, is she? But what do I care? What do I have to do with her? See, that's what the world's like – nothing to do with me, mate, get them dealt with, we're not interested in come-backs, none of that, move on. Take, take, take, well not me, sir, oh no, I'm not a taker of everything and fuck everyone. I'm putting my own shit aside to go visit V, see what is going on.

I put my coat on and closed the curtains. The breeze and snow was still getting in, and as much as I'd like to sit hand and hand with Old Storm watching a Christmas Carol, it didn't fit, and if V comes back with me, the place will have to be warm otherwise she might as well be out there at the mercy of the scumbags. And it is Christmas Eve. Christmas Eve! Oh, I love Christmas Eve and so should V. With Old Storm and V, we're going to have a party, smoke a few joints and take it easy.

23

When I got outside the sky was full. It took me back to when V and me first came out. Do you remember? Did I write that bit down? I hope so. Anyway, that's where I was right now, except she wasn't here. I looked up and the curtains were sucked into the flat and it looked terrible. I stepped back and took my chin off my chest and let the snow gush down my top.

In the park, I turned and looked back at my flat, and again my heart started thumping. I took my hand out of my pocket and put it on my chest to feel it. Like a test. Look here Tyler, this is how you really feel, not what you think. It was upsetting seeing my curtains blowing in there, the flat deserted. Is this how I was going to leave it – just walk away right now? A broken window, broken landing light, leaking tap, phone cut off – this broken flat can't hold me any longer.

The contents of the flat started going through my mind, like on some game show hosted by a corpse with grey hair and false teeth. Try and remember these, Tyler... a 9-Bar, nice prize for any dossers passing that see the window and get in. A magazine, my coffee table – surely that has sell on value, it's worth a few quid, and then that's it. Nothing else worth going back for. Even if there was, I wouldn't set foot in the place ever again. It's brought me to my knees. It's the bubble that's been keeping me fucked these past couple of days, and that's all it's been, you know. I'm sure that's as long as it's been, like I said I was working at the start of the week, took a day off to talk to that shrink, and now this.

As I stood there, I was getting more and more fascinated by the flat. This was like a new me watching the old me and I could see all the comings and goings. No one today and who could blame them in this weather. In the past all the dope-heads coming for their fix.

I'm picturing me, sprawled out on the settee, and the bell going. What the fuckers didn't realise was that I checked out the window before I went downstairs to the spy hole. If there was anyone there, even halfway down the street, I wouldn't answer the door. This was the way it was, and it worked well. And look at it now, Old Storm wrecking the place – good enough for it, I say.

I got to the top of the bank and had a feeling of being all warm – a full belly, things were looking up, and on I went knowing that my time in the flat was now gone

I got to the first doorway and checked in my pockets for some cash. I had eight pound. Not bad at all. I also had Nut-job's card.

I stood in the doorway of the Hot Oven Café. Café-cum bakery, you know, like Greggs, except this housed all the old biddies in the back who bought scones and cuppas and put the world to rights. The place was full and I got a whiff of sausage rolls. Sausage rolls or pasties, and I thought, You're going to have to eat, so in I went and stood in the queue.

24

Not sure how long I had stood there but the queue decided to stop moving and I was right across the entrance to the café so I had to keep stepping forward and letting the old dears past. What a carry-on, and they kept thanking me and all the while I'm thinking, Get fucking past for fuck's sakes and let me out of here.

It was too busy, too much going on and the idiot causing the hold-up was a fat bald bloke, big hanging chops and I couldn't help it, and I tried looking away, but where is there to look in a queue apart from straight ahead? The racket coming of the old fucker was unbelievable, and I had a woman about six inches tall with a plastic thing on her head huffing and puffing, and I'm getting hotter and hotter with all my gear on, but not wanting to take my hat off or lower my scarf.

I was starting to feel sick, like I needed to rest on something, and then the volume went down and I couldn't hear anything at all and I was staring at this bloke, and I've never seen a neck like it, the amount of flesh hanging. It was like a dipping washing line starting at his chin and I was on my hundredth flash of me pulling his head back and gutting him and leaving him gasping on the floor with his buns, when the volume came back on and a woman, tall thing, about V's age, stepped forward a few places and put her hand on my arm. She asked if I was alright and if I needed a glass of water, and I looked around at the rest of the people in there, and the bloke had stopped arguing, and the woman behind the counter was looking at me... and I was off, out the door, close to bursting and I ran down the road, fast as I could and out into the open.

A crowd of smudges were coming down the street and I didn't have the energy to run. I couldn't move, so I sunk down the wall and sat there. I pulled my scarf up over my face and kept looking at the ground until they passed.

As they walked past, they didn't even notice me. Like I was invisible. I looked up. Across the road people were the same, old woman and her man, locked together, hurried past me like I wasn't there.

When there was no one around, I pushed myself up and walked down the bank, thinking, why didn't anyone help me up? They tried to help me in the bakers, but when I'd keeled over, I became invisible to them.

I kept on walking and I started to feel all invisible like the Invisible Man, and how good would that be? I got so excited I had to run, and the only placed for running in this weather was the park, so off I went, jogging along thinking about being the Invisible Man, you know the bit with the scarf? I mean, how good would that be? Being invisible, no one seeing you, only you seeing them, and as I was thinking that I passed Dave C's the barbers, and I thought about being an invisible barber, except I'd be the Demon Barber, and my chair would be in the middle of the park and you'd get sent down to me when Dave C was full and in the chair I'd spin you around and around and ask what you want, and you'd be looking about thinking, Where the fuck's this barber? By the time you answered, I'd glide across the floor and everything I'd been fighting against I'd let go and slit your throat and you'd be flapping around in the snow, what a fucking scene! Can you imagine the colour of the red on the white and the shapes and colours and all the while I'm cleaning my cut-throat, Old Storm is covering you over. The art is there, and then it's gone. Now you see it, now you don't. People would come to the barber's chair in the park late at night, the junkies would have a shot and ZIP, they'd stagger into the lake Old Storm and me, like the ghosts of Christmas past, would whip

around them telling them the perils of taking drugs.
Invisible is what I needed to be.

25

I made my way across town, dropping my invisible trick whenever there were too many people around. Here's a funny one for you: – before I go on, what do you make of that colon? Not poncy like the semicolon. Nice and hard, like it tells you proper what the score is. If it's so fucking clever, why not use a full stop? The Big Daddy. When the full stop is in town, there's no doubt what you have to do. Colon? 50-50.

So, here's a funny one for you: when I sat down on the corner of Blanch Ave an old dear was passing and she dropped me a fiver! A fiver in my lap like I was a beggar, and I wanted to say, Don't be fucking ridiculous, I've got a 9-bar in the house to punt, but I couldn't, so I nodded, and wished I'd been wearing fingerless gloves, because that was the scene, all Oliver Twist again, and me the one with no legs looking for some bread. What a scene. Now you see me, now you don't.

It might as well have been midnight it was so

dark and cold. The snow had turned nasty, coming down at an angle and with the weight of the wise-one behind it, it was taking no prisoners, me included.

I was in the doorway of a travel shop. Lunn Poly or some shit place, they're all the same. They all rip you off and have special deals on then fuck you over when you have a complaint. No decency, like estate agents. Fuck the lot of them. Anyway, the young woman, lady, you might say, spotted me through the side window, and all very casual like, drew the blinds. Made me laugh, and I got up and walked up the road, making good progress.

When I got to Port Terrace, a part of town I'd never been to before, or at least I can't remember ever coming this far over, I sat on a wall opposite Nut-job's office. I wasn't sure if he'd be working Christmas Eve. Probably had money to burn and didn't need to, but it was worth checking. His office was the bottom one in a row of terraces. They looked like they should be posh student flats, you know, white brick, years old, listed or some shit, except they were all offices, I reckon.

Next door to him were solicitors, somebody and somebody incorporating somebody. I couldn't make out the next one along, then I realised I had been spotted by Nut-job. He was at the bottom window, arms folded. Black hair, beige jumper, plain as a digestive biscuit. That made me laugh. He would fall apart if dunked in tea.

I walked away like I hadn't seen him and went round the corner to think things through because I wasn't feeling as bad as I had when I'd left the flat, and maybe I didn't need him anymore, just a clean break to get myself back together. That's what I needed. But what difference would it make if I popped in to see him? And wasn't it down to him to sort that side of things out? I thought about last night when I rang him, and the alternative of my parents finding out, and I nearly chucked up right there on the pavement.

I was on a corner, at a set of traffic lights and I noticed for the first time that cars were passing. Slowly, but they were passing and opposite, further up the road, a car was sideways on. You're not going to beat Old Storm if he doesn't want to be beaten.

Thinking that filled me full of confidence, and with him whistling around my ears I thought, You know what? He's brought you here, like he took you to the park last night, and now you're here, so take the advice and go see Nut-job. So I did.

26

There was a footpath running along the front of the terraced offices so you could walk from one to the other. As I got so far along, I thought about running straight past and down the street and away. I wanted to be back outside the flat with my hand outside my pocket, holding my chest, feeling all warm and full again, but all I could think of was being inside, except this was worse than the flat or the hospital because this was Nut-job's place and he was all-seeing and hearing and he could see through me and see what was going on and he had the power to send me away and into the most clinical and coldest place of them all, because they never let you die, just pump you full of anti-depressants to keep you alive and then you're forgotten about and there's no coming out and they might even cut your brain out because it's hereditary, like they did on Cuckoo's Nest, and I didn't want that because I knew I was only out of sorts and just needed a little pick-me-up and this was the last place to go before it blew right open, and my parents and brother and sister, saying they knew something was up and they blamed it on this and that but what did they know? They didn't even know me, and now all this trouble at the door, and the neighbours, what would they think, and all the while, all I wanted was some peace.

I wasn't giving in, not me. I could easily give in, and I'm not sure what happens after that, if I give in, whether they take me away. It could be easily treatable. I'm thinking all this shit and it's far too much and I can feel the bile rising when Nut-job comes out the door and he's within a foot of me. If he grabbed at me he would have a hold, and then what?

Nut-job offered me his hand and my stomach dropped when I accepted it. It felt like I had just stepped off a cliff, the wind was rushing past me and I'm looking up and thinking, This is the life, watch me go, free as a bird and I'm never coming back and what speed, past branches, rock faces, seas, I'm heading south and I plunge into the water and go deeper and deeper, my coat coming off, away it goes, off with my top and I can see under water, crystal clear, and I'm swimming with not a stitch on, and I'm not bothered and I see it ahead, and slightly stiffen up, then it comes closer, the nose of a shark or dolphin and I instantly know it's friendly, it's a dolphin and I grab onto its fin and it pulls me deeper and deeper, into dark blue and I'm feeling colder and colder, not wanting to be there and I tap him on the nose. Up mate, up until we're in the sunshine, and up we go and we rush through the water, tearing through it and we both come out together up into the sky and I leap off with a dive and there are more dolphins around me. I'm surrounded and we're all friends and we're all safe and the cliff face is white, and there's a cave and the adventure looks like it's just beginning, and we're all free as we want to be, no faces, no crowds, miles of ocean up and down, side to side, better than the park, better than anywhere because no matter how far you go and in any direction, you never touch a thing...

Nut-job snaps me out of it with a piping hot cup of tea. All-time cure of any problems. He's all smiles, and I apologise, mumbling like a fucking idiot, about disturbing him on Christmas Eve, and he gives me the over-exaggerated, What you on about look, and picks the calendar up of his desk. It's one of those calendars that are in a triangle, and it's got a cliff and a bird on it, like in my day-dream, and it'll have his name on probably –

Doctor Nut-job, don't mind sectioning you, even on Christmas Eve.

He looked at the calendar and said I was a few weeks ahead of myself, and it was only the 14th of December. I felt all funny then, thinking I'd got that wrong, but with me not being at work and in the house, no papers, and all that, it was an easy mistake. It's not like it's the middle of June, we're only talking ten days. I've been on one since I left work, so yeah, I'll take that one, he's one up and we haven't even got through the fucking pleasantries.

He's sitting opposite me, on the edge of his seat at first, then he leans back, crossing his legs and all the time I'm looking at him and his words are floating about between us, nothing really registering because if the truth be known I couldn't give a fuck what he has to say, not unless he can tell me why I'm sitting here and fighting the urge to pick that ash tray up and smash him in the face with it.

Then it started. The noise drifting past, like a boat avoiding a rock in the water, then it changes course and goes around. The sound is like that, coming my way, then slips past my ears, getting further away and all I can concentrate on is the other person's lips moving, like you see on a film when they home in on the face.

Here we go again, I'm homing in. I can see his teeth, the black lines, he's a smoker and he's got plenty to say and I can't hear anything and I'm getting closer, my breathing harder, and I want to edge along the seat. I focus on the glass ashtray. Why is it here if you can't smoke? I look away from what he's saying and I notice it's not an ashtray at all.

I was starting to feel sick and I couldn't watch his mouth a second longer, so I slid down the chair and onto the floor. I kicked the chair back and now I'm looking up at him and he was talking over the top of the ashtray, which wasn't an ashtray but a small vase.

On the floor, I could speak to him, like he wasn't really there, and I told him straight, I told him I was having nasty thoughts, but I didn't think I'd ever act on them. Trying to be all professional I was, because I knew he had certain powers. I was fighting the tears back thinking, I want to go in, but if only I knew what they did. I couldn't hold the tears back and he stopped talking, then I got it together again.

Nut asked if I wanted another drink, and it was the way he said it, and we both knew what he was going to do and I bolted for the door, with my name coming from his mouth echoing around and I couldn't go through with it because I hadn't done anything wrong and I didn't know what they would do to me and I didn't deserve that.

27

When I stopped running I was way up on the other side of town, walking up a high street, and Old Storm had helped me all the way. I was tiring and the street was getting full, far too many people and I was getting funny looks for dallying about and I needed to be invisible again so I dropped down in the first doorway.

I came too some time later and I felt like I was swimming with the dolphins. I took my scarf off and looked up and not one person looked at me. No one looked at me and I had never been happier. I breathed in, all relaxed. I didn't want to stay in this doorway, but until I could figure things out, it was the best place to be, and I felt like setting up home, you know, getting my spices out and making a go of it, so I huddled in for the night.

When the morning came I moved on, real quick before anyone was about, and when it got busy in the next town I dropped down into the ocean again. By mid afternoon I was making a few quid sticking my coffee cup out and it made me giddy as hell when a coin dropped in. I swear you didn't have to look at where it came from and there was no need to say a word, and I kept thinking of V and wondering if she was okay.

Anyway, this is where I'm at and you've probably just passed me and not bothered dropping me a bean, you tight fucker. Well come back! Only joking. This is where I'm at now and I've made it through to Monday and I'm going to figure things out and I think writing it down has been a help. When I'm back on my feet, I'm going re-write this proper, all professional and maybe I can read it one day and realise what's happened.

*For more information on Street,
Tyler Stevens and Paperbooks
Publishing, visit:*

www.legendpress.co.uk

More from Paperbooks Publishing

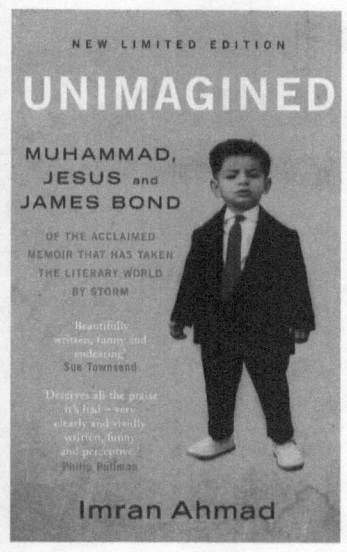

Unimagined
Imran Ahmad

The beguiling memoir that has taken the literary world by storm, with an astonishing list of endorsements and touching the hearts of readers all of over the world.

Both deliciously funny and deeply insightful, *Unimagined* is the true story of a Muslim boy growing up torn between his Islamic identity and his desire to embrace the West. Join Imran on his struggle against corruption and injustice, his eternal quest to be the quintessential English gentleman (The Saint), his yearning for the coolest car (Jaguar XJS), and his desire for the perfect girlfriend (preferably brunette, but any kind considered).

ISBN: 9781907756320 Hardback £13.99

More from Paperbooks Publishing

Sons and Fascination
G.S. Mattu

Jack meets with Francesca, a woman older than him by some years and is immediately captivated by her. However, her presence at his father's club in a pulsing London has a scandalous story he's not aware of. And, even though she in turns falls for Jack, the truth must eventually emerge.

Jack's world unravels as all those around him face up to the impossibility of escaping your own self. With everything changed, fraught relationships and lives must be brought back from the brink or left to dust.

ISBN: 9781907756009 Hardback £7.99

More from Paperbooks Publishing

The Grease Monkey's Tale
Paul Burman

For Nic the mechanic, life is becoming a journey of stories: good, bad, happy and sad. When Siobhan McConnell hurtles into his world, Nic's life bounces between tragedy, romance and thriller.

Framed for armed robbery, it seems he's on the brink of losing everything until he's offered the 'job-of-a-lifetime' in the remote township of Gimbly, where very little is what it seems to be. Nic starts to discover a devastating truth but should he learn to live with what he finds, or take action to shake the town to its very core?

ISBN: 9781907461163 Paperback £7.99